2

D1436412

a30118 015605490b

Trepidation in Downing Street

Trepidation in Downing Street

and other Stories

by

L. E. Jones

Rupert Hart-Davis
36 Soho Square
1962

© L. E. Jones 1962

PRINTED AND BOUND IN ENGLAND BY
HAZELL WATSON AND VINEY LTD
AYLESBURY AND SLOUGH

Contents

Acknowledgement

"The Goat," as any Norfolk reader will recognise, is an old story expanded and embroidered in the re-telling.

Trepidation in Downing Street

IT was the job of Mr Cyril Cuffe, the junior and least important of the Prime Minister's Secretaries, to open all the letters, except those marked "Private," which arrived daily at Number 10 Downing Street. Having opened them, he had to decide which must be passed on to one or other of the Senior Secretaries, and which to deal with himself. The task needed discretion because, as he had early discovered, it was as easy to get his head snapped off for passing on too little as for passing on too much. Being a self-confident young man, his natural inclination was to shoulder responsibility, while that of his colleagues was to opine that young Cuffe was too big for his boots.

About a letter, however, that arrived one morning with the postmark "Douglas, Isle of Man," he had no hesitation. It was addressed to the Prime Minister himself; it was headed "Seaview, Port Soderick"; and it was written in the moderately legible hand of an educated and well-bred man.

The letter was as follows:

Dear Mr Prime Minister,

After forty years' confinement in what is called a Voluntary Home for the Mentally Afflicted, I have, at the age of sixty, been finally discharged as cured. (My own view is that I never was mentally afflicted, but that is neither here nor there, besides being too long a story.) The thing about me which I think will interest you is that, besides sharing your not so uncommon name, I am the living image of yourself. This striking resemblance, while a cause of amusement to my friends and sometimes of excitement to strangers, did not seem to me to be of any use or interest until I happened to see, a few days ago in Douglas, a film about a man who was the "double" of General Montgomery ("Monty," I suspect, to both of us). It appears that in the late war this chance resemblance was put to very good purpose, with the result that a private individual, with nothing in particular to recommend him beyond his likeness to a great man, was enabled to serve his country effectively.

Now, sir, we are no longer at war, but it appears to me that the Prime Minister, with a "double" at his disposal, is likely to find many occasions when it would be to his own and even to the nation's advantage for him to be in two places at once. It goes without saying that the double must be only seen and not heard, but there must be occasions where the mere presence of the Prime Minister could give pleasure to many, and thereby increase his popularity and the prestige of his Government.

Accordingly, sir, I now offer you my services. I am a man of means, and ask for no emoluments. I propose to make my headquarters in London, where I shall live effectively disguised, indoors and out, except on those occasions when you instruct me to be mistaken for yourself.

For sixty years of my life, sir, which has spanned two great wars, I have been prevented from rendering the least service to my country. The strength of my desire to be of some use, so long as you continue to hold your high office, will, I hope and trust, be an earnest of my obedience, discretion and reliability.

Yours truly

Andrew Smith.

Cyril Cuffe read the letter through once, and tossed it into a large wicker waste-paper basket known as the "loony-bin." He was to live to regret that he had not made a note of the address at the head of the letter. After the lapse of about three weeks a second letter in the same handwriting was delivered to 10 Downing Street, and opened by Cuffe. This time the envelope bore a London postmark, but there was no address on the letter itself. It ran as follows:

Dear Mr Prime Minister,

Twenty days have passed since I wrote to you offering you my services (unpaid) as your "double." As you have not replied, not even, as I had expected, to ask for my photograph, I can only conclude that my proposal does not interest you.

It interests me, however, very much. So much so that I have decided, off my own bat, to impersonate you in such places and on such occasions as will, I sincerely trust, enable me to increase the public goodwill towards yourself and the Conservative party.

Yours truly

Andrew Smith.

This time Cyril Cuffe scratched his head. He rather wished that he had noted the address on the first letter. No doubt the man was a lunatic, but it would have been more prudent to ask for his photograph and judge whether his likeness to the Prime Minister was of a kind that could conceivably lead to an awkward situation. Should he consult Littlejohn, the senior Private Secretary? He decided against it. For what could be done? Even if the man could be traced through the Isle of Man police, it was no crime to look like the Prime Minister. And he was too well-off to be bought. He decided to do nothing, and the second letter was also thrown into the loony-bin.

It should be mentioned here that the Prime Minister, the Right Honourable Andrew Smith, was a man of striking appearance. It was sometimes said that not since Mr Gladstone had a Prime Minister been equipped with such notable and distinguished features. His nose was a larger edition of the Duke of Wellington's. His eyebrows outdid the late Sir Arthur

Pinero's. His chin jutted. His clean-shaven face was deeply lined. He was tall and upright. In short, he was unmistakable. The caricaturists had nothing to do but draw him to the life. Mr Cuffe could be pardoned for thinking that nature could hardly have cast a second Andrew Smith in so idiosyncratic a mould. But Mr Cuffe, although pardonable, was wrong.

A few days after the delivery of the second letter a junior head of the hydra-headed "Waterloo," the social and political columnist of the *Daily Echo*, was rung up from a call-box. A polite and well-bred voice informed him that if he cared to go to early service at St Martin-in-the-Fields daily in the following week, he might find it journalistically rewarding. There was something about the tone of voice of the caller, a kind of quiet confidence in the advice he was proffering, that decided the young journalist, much as he disliked early rising, to give St Martin-in-the-Fields a chance. The church had been "news" in the past, and might be "news" again.

At half-past seven on Monday morning he accordingly took a modest seat in a back pew of St Martin's. What he saw there determined him, with the help of an alarm-clock, to repeat his visit on the following day. Again rewarded, he completed, as advised by his mysterious caller, a whole week of church-going.

On the ensuing Monday Mr Derek Littlejohn was chatting, in a brief interlude of work, with his Chief.

"Have you seen 'Waterloo' this morning, sir?"

"You know I never look at 'Waterloo'."

"But you generally manage to know of anything he has written. I think this might amuse you."

And Littlejohn took from his note-case a cutting, which he handed to the Prime Minister. It ran as follows:

It appears that even his closest friends are not aware of the Prime Minister's custom of attending Early Morning Service daily, at the early hour of half-past seven, at St Martin-in-the-Fields. When I asked the Vicar, the Rev. Luke Allgood, whether this had been a long-standing habit of Mr Smith's, he told me, genially but firmly, that he never discussed members of his congregation.

"Well I'm damned," said the Prime Minister. "To think that I was considering him for Hereford! People always say he's so straightforward. Why couldn't he tell the truth? I've never been to St Martin's in my life, except for a memorial service or two! You can scratch him off that short list."

"I suppose he hoped to attract a few more customers," said Littlejohn.

"I don't care what he hoped. He won't do for a bishop."

"Do you want me to put 'Waterloo' right, sir?"

The Prime Minister considered for a moment.

"If we're always to be putting the Press right there'll be no end to it. It's not as if it was libellous. A lot of people will be pleased. Remember Halifax in India? Did him no end of good. I should leave it alone."

"You know best, sir."

So Littlejohn left it alone. The Vicar of St Martin's lost his chance of the see of Hereford, but he did, for a week or so, have larger congregations at his early services. And quite a number of voters were genuinely touched by reading of the Prime Minister's unexpected devotions. There were friendly comments in all the church, and not a few other, newspapers. And in his comfortable Bayswater flat, where he was never seen without a heavy false moustache and a pair of massive spectacles (exchanged, out of doors, for dark glasses), the other Andrew Smith, his round-shouldered figure bending over his press-cuttings, was more than satisfied.

About a week after the appearance of "Waterloo's" paragraph the Prime Minister was confined to the house for a couple of days with a chill. About five o'clock on the second afternoon a telegram was brought to Cyril Cuffe. He read it and handed it, looking slightly shell-shocked, to Littlejohn, who in turn took it, looking wholly shell-shocked, to the Prime Minister, peacefully drinking tea with Mrs Smith in her sitting-room. The telegram, which was in French, was translated by Mrs Smith as follows:

> Profoundly touched and moved, dear friend, by your incomparable gesture. In thanking you from the depth of my heart, I speak, believe me, for all France. De Gaulle.

For all its warmth, it was not an easy or comfortable telegram for a statesman to receive at tea-time, especially at a moment when relations with the General were slightly strained, particularly when the recipient had made no gesture, public or private, of any kind. The Prime Minister was even more profoundly puzzled than the sender of the message had been touched and moved. Could it be a hoax? He could hardly ring up the French President to enquire whether he had sent a telegram to Downing Street that afternoon.

After an irritable discussion Littlejohn was told to ring up the British Embassy in Paris and see whether they could throw any light upon the mystery. But before he could get through, Downing Street was rung up by the *Evening Gazette*. Littlejohn took the call. The Editor himself was on the line.

"Is the Prime Minister back yet?"

"What do you mean 'back'?"

"From Rouen, of course. We've just had the whole story from our Paris man, but of course we should appreciate anything you can give us from your end. Especially the reason for the secrecy. Jolly good show, anyway. They say the General's purring like a cat. Do no end of good. We've just sent to the airport for the photographs. But if you could just tell us how the Old Man got there, and how he got back—if he is back?"

"He's here, all right."

"Good. So what can we say?"

"That's for him to decide. Hardly had a word with him yet. I'll ring you later."

"Thank you—and, once again, congratulations!"

Littlejohn went back to the Prime Minister's room.

"That was the *Gazette*, sir. You've been to Rouen today. And de Gaulle's purring like a cat. So the wire's genuine all right."

"Why Rouen?"

"As there's nobody we dare ask, sir, I suppose we shall have to wait for the morning papers. There are to be photographs in them."

At that moment the call to the British Embassy came through. Littlejohn again took it. The Ambassador was on the line. He began speaking at once.

"I was just going to ring you up," he said, "but I wasn't sure whether the Prime Minister would be home yet. I'm afraid he may have been wondering why I wasn't there. But the General himself insisted that this was to be a domestic affair—for Frenchmen only—that was why the Prime Minister's appearance has made such a stir: a stroke of genius, if I may so. Of course, between you and me, Littlejohn, it might have been a good plan to tip me the wink beforehand—but not a word to the P.M. about that. It's merely that I've been feeling rather an ass with the French press."

"I can sympathise with you, Your Excellency," said Littlejohn, thinking it would have been a good plan if his Chief and himself had been tipped the wink beforehand.

"Well, I mustn't keep you," said the Ambassador. "Just make it clear that the Embassies were all asked to stay away. That's all."

"Certainly, Your Excellency." And Paris rang off. Littlejohn went to Cuffe's room.

"Get yesterday's French papers from the F.O. or anywhere you like. And be quick about it. There was some 'do' at Rouen today with de Gaulle. It must have been mentioned."

Cuffe could hustle at need, and it was not long before he brought some French newspapers to Littlejohn, half-distracted with telephone-callers from the press, from Paris, from the Foreign Office, all of whom must, from such replies as the unhappy man could contrive, have thought that the Prime Minister's senior Private Secretary had lost his wits.

The French papers all mentioned that, on the following day,

at noon, General de Gaulle was to unveil, at Rouen, a new gigantic statue of Joan of Arc, subscribed for by his admirers.

"There seems to be no doubt that you were there, sir," he said to the Prime Minister.

"But I wasn't," said that harassed man. He read de Gaulle's telegram again. "Or was I? Do you know, Derek, I'm beginning to think that I shall have to have been there."

"It was what I was thinking too," said Littlejohn.

"It's a blessing I've been in all day," said the Prime Minister.

"Exactly what I was thinking," said Littlejohn.

Both had a sleepless night.

Cuffe was the first to see the morning papers. The photographs of the ceremony at Rouen were unusually clear. Some showed the Prime Minister, in morning dress and with a grey top hat in his hand, standing within a few yards of the platform from which General de Gaulle was speaking. Others showed him bending to lay a wreath of bay-leaves at the foot of the huge modernistic statue of the Maid, seated, in full armour, upon a mountainous stone Percheron. There was a picture of his hinder-parts as he climbed into a black limousine—but this one was hardly evidence. Only one morning paper, the *Daily Hooter*, carried a first-hand account of the affair, and this was thanks to a mysterious telephone message, delivered in a polite, well-bred voice, from a call-box, informing them that a visit to Rouen on the following day would well repay them. It seems that only at the last moment before General de Gaulle began to speak did the British Prime Minister step quietly out of the crowd into the small, sunlit space in front of the platform. There he stood, his magnificent nose tilted upwards, gazing steadfastly, with affectionate eyes, at the speaker. He listened, with no perceptible diminution of affection in his regard, to the story, eloquently and dramatically told, of how his countrymen had been thrashed and driven out of France by the Maid. And when the speech ended, during the deafening applause which ensued, he took a few steps forward and laid a great wreath of bay-laurel, deftly handed to him by a chauffeur, at the foot of the statue. The General, who, apart from the journalists and cameramen, was one of the few to recognise the conspicuous but unexpected figure below him, stretched out a hand, permitted himself to smile, and even took a step in the direction of the stooping figure. But the Prime Minister straightened himself, and without so much as a glance towards the platform, disappeared into the crowd. It was an amateur at the back of the cheering mob who secured and sold to the Press the snapshot of one of the first behinds in England.

The consternation felt that morning in Downing Street was almost more than the men's well-trained features could cope with; Mrs Smith's face crumpled and she wept. To discover that you have a double as like as an identical twin may be amusing or embarrassing; but when you are Prime Minister and your double takes advantage of that fact to play a prominent part in the delicate sphere of foreign relations, the discovery is flabbergasting. There is no laughing it off, nor, when the double has succeeded in cajoling the formidable French President into such a telegram (reported in full in all the morning papers), is there any to whom it would be safe to explain the truth. The Foreign Minister, the Ambassador, the Cabinet—all must be kept in the dark. And worse, some explanation must be offered to them as to why their leader should have made, entirely off his own bat, so sudden, so secret, so unconventional a raid across the Channel.

But if the Prime Minister, his wife, Littlejohn and Perkins (the second secretary) were almost at their wits' end, poor Cyril Cuffe was in even worse case. For to him had been given due notice, not only of the double's existence, but of his intention to make public use of his resemblance to the great man. And not only that, but Cuffe had wantonly thrown away, and forgotten, an address in the Isle of Man that would have enabled them to approach and conciliate the ridiculous fellow. That he would be amenable to persuasion was certain, for his letters had been written from a wish to be helpful. The wretched Cuffe decided that he must make a clean breast to his chief.

And he did. The Prime Minister's relief at hearing that the man's name was known, and that he had been living a few weeks earlier in the Isle of Man, was so great that Cuffe's negligence was, for the time being, overlooked. The police were sent for and told that they must, for no reason given, at all costs trace a Mr Andrew Smith, aged about sixty, who had lately inhabited the Isle of Man after forty years in a Home for the Mentally Afflicted. For the Douglas police to track down Seaview was almost too easy. But there the scent ended. Mr Smith's housekeeper informed them that her master had left on a voyage round the world, and only important letters were to be forwarded to Poste Restante, Tokyo. In the light of this intelligence, the gravity of Cuffe's misdemeanour became apparent, and only his privity to the ghastly secret saved him from dismissal.

It was Cuffe who suggested a hidden message to the double in the personal columns of *The Times* and other newspapers. It ran as follows: "Andrew S. Will the gentleman who in April last so kindly offered his services as stand-in communicate at once with Box etc."

Mr Andrew Smith, of the heavy moustache and the dark glasses, did not miss this message, for he had expected something of the sort. But an approach which, after his mild success in St Martin-in-the-Fields, would have given him much pleasure, now failed to interest him. For the resounding success, on both sides of the Channel, of his appearance at Rouen had turned his head. Why, he asked himself, had not the Prime Minister or his advisers thought of so simple, so effective a means of touching the hearts of the gesture-loving French? The answer must be, of course, that they lacked the imagination, the social deftness, of himself, Andrew Smith. If he were now, in response to this invitation in the Agony Columns, to put himself at the disposal of No. 10 Downing Street, it would be a case of the better serving the worse. It was little wonder that they should want him there, but he had no intention, most decidedly he had no intention, of taking orders from people who so little understood their own business.

No replies were received to Mr Cuffe's message.

The Prime Minister, tortured with shame at the lies he had been compelled to tell his colleagues, and squirming beneath the fulsome compliments of the Press, both at home and abroad, was losing his sleep and even his nerve. He had panicky visions of opening his papers one morning to find that he had committed his country, at unheralded conferences at the White House or the Kremlin, to the most unheard-of solutions of God knows what problems.

He need not have worried. His double's head may have been turned, but it was still firmly screwed on. Mr Andrew Smith was well aware that a conjunction like that of the Rouen affair, when the Prime Minister's indisposition coincided with a sentimental occasion within easy helicopter-range, would recur infrequently, if at all. He knew that he could go into action only when two indispensable conditions were present: the Prime Minister out of sight and himself under no necessity to speak. Such occasions were not likely to be common. In the meantime, while fully realising the advantages of calling in the press as witnesses to his doings, he thought it provident to retain a private photographer. He was fortunate in finding a young man sufficiently honest and amused to serve him faithfully. The tenterhooks in Downing Street were becoming a thought blunter, by use, when the newspapers carried snapshots, on the day after the Derby, of the Prime Minister standing in a queue at the door of a betting-shop. The captions were, for the most part, friendly if facetious. The Prime Minister himself, who had never made a bet in his life, was decidedly put out, but Littlejohn, who ran an account with Ladbroke's, was able to reassure him.

'None of the people it will shock ever did, or ever will, vote Conservative, sir. It will only do you good with the mass of the faithful. I'm beginning to think your double knows his job."

The next picture to appear in the press was taken by flashlight, and sent to the papers with a note that "it represented an occasion some time ago." It showed the Prime Minister, in full evening dress, dining tête-à-tête at a small table with an immense, motherly and jovial Negress. Its appearance was opportune. The Prime Minister had been most unfairly accused in the House of personal prejudice against black people. Here was the answer for all to see. The age and proportions of the lady precluded any suggestion of impropriety, and the publication of the picture actually prompted an apology from the offending member of the Opposition.

"Double's still doing well," commented Littlejohn.

"That's all very well for you," said the Prime Minister, "but I've got to account for the black beauty to my colleagues and friends."

"Say she was in your service when you were in North Africa during the war," said Littlejohn.

"Lies upon lies!" said the unhappy statesman. But say it he did.

For Mr Andrew Smith the thing had been almost too easy. He had found in his pocket-book the address, in Ealing, of a retired Jamaican nurse who had looked after him for many years in the Home for the Mentally Afflicted. It was a red-letter day for her when her old patient, now recovered, invited her to dine with him in his Bayswater flat, dressed himself up to the nines in her honour, and insisted on recording the occasion with a flashlight photograph taken by an amused and obliging young friend of her host.

Fate played into Mr Smith's hands when the Prime Minister, after a bout of summer flu, was advised by his doctors to take ten days' complete rest at Bognor Regis. To the Prime Minister, who liked sea-air but detested beach-life, a rest meant the shady gardens of The Towers, a Victorian villa secluded by Victorian shrubberies and standing back at least a mile from the sea. And, except for an occasional motor-drive over the downs into the weald, the Prime Minister spent his holiday in a garden-chair, re-reading *Vanity Fair*.

But to the public a seaside holiday meant the beach, and they followed, with sympathetic interest, the various stages of the Prime Minister's convalescence in the picture papers. For the first day or two the snapshots showed him reclining in a silk dressing-gown, at full length upon the sands. But the celebrated air of Bognor soon began to tell, and in no time the great man was seen disporting himself, in a boldly striped bathing-suit, in the sea itself. Feeling more active still, he sculled himself in a dinghy, or played single-wicket cricket on the sands with two small boys who afterwards shocked the local reporter by confessing that they had no idea what a Prime Minister was. He appeared to have had a slight relapse the day he slept soundly under a beach-umbrella, while visitors tip-toed about him with their Kodaks, but on the following day he was attempting to ride an inflated rubber horse, huge, bulbous and bright yellow, in the surf. On the last day he ran, and won, a fifty-yard race with a small girl to whom he gave thirty yards start.

Mr Andrew Smith had been enabled to enjoy this carefree holiday on Bognor sands because his tame photographer, calling politely at The Towers on the day of the Prime Minister's arrival, had been told that the distinguished convalescent's privacy must be respected, and that he would not be visiting the town or the beach.

But to Littlejohn, Perkins and Cuffe, in Downing Street, the daily appearances of the double in public seemed to offer a rare opportunity for approaching, and coming to terms with, the cause of such continuing apprehension, not to say demoralisation, in the mind of the Queen's First Minister. Of the double's general goodwill they felt assured; surely they had only to explain to him the terrible consequences of some false step or miscalculation on his part, to persuade him to call it a day. They decided not to trouble their Chief with the matter (and in fact Mrs Smith was taking care to keep the daily pictures out of his sight) but to act on their own. It was decided that Littlejohn should go down to Bognor and tackle Mr Smith on the beach. If by chance the Press should take a snapshot of the double in conversation with the Prime Minister's Private Secretary, what could be more natural than that?

On the day of his arrival at Bognor Littlejohn, although he spent the whole day in the ferocious glare, which he loathed, of a white, south-facing beach, drew blank. For Mr Andrew Smith, in spite of the assurance given to his photographer at The Towers, was taking no risks, and was careful to be out of sight and heavily moustached in his lodgings before ten o'clock each morning. Littlejohn, however, who knew nothing of the guarantee given to the photographer, was acute enough to guess how the double's mind would be working, and on the following day he was on the beach at eight o'clock. By nine he was sitting, back to a breakwater, in friendly talk with Mr Smith.

Littlejohn's greeting to the man he was looking for had been: "Hullo, sir, I'd no idea you would be up and about so early!" because, face to face, he felt sure that it was to the Prime Minister himself that he was speaking. But Mr Smith's polite "Good morning" put him right. The voice was the voice of Jacob.

Their talk was long and amicable. But Mr Smith was quite firm on one point: he was not going to retire from the game. He spoke movingly of his long years of frustration in the Home for the Mentally Afflicted; of how he had never been in a position to render his country the slightest service; of how he had now created for himself an opportunity of making up for the lost years by a selfless dedication to the cause of the Conservative party and consequently of the nation. He challenged Littlejohn to deny that, hitherto, his activities had been beneficial and, in the Rouen affair, of international importance.

Littlejohn granted him everything, but pointed out how the very éclat of the Rouen adventure aggravated the terrors of a chance discovery that the Prime Minister possessed an identical double. Once that was known, some sleuth in the Opposition press would be certain to get on to the scent. The Prime Minister would be committed to further perjuries, and God knew where it would end. Mr Smith pooh-poohed his fears: what he had done once he could, he felt sure, do again. Littlejohn was beginning to think that he must now play his last card, and disclose to this over-confident egoist the abject private miseries of his Chief, when a new thought struck him. If Mr Smith should be ultimately persuaded to forgo his cherished activities, the discovery that the Prime Minister had a double would be, not a dreadful possibility, but a dead certainty. For it could hardly be demanded of the man, in addition to the sacrifice of his chosen vocation, that he should for ever appear in public in a false moustache and dark glasses, or alternatively emigrate to Brazil.

Inwardly tremulous at the thought of how near he might have been, had Smith been less stubborn, to putting the fat into the fire, but outwardly placid, Littlejohn now reverted to the double's original offer, in his first letters, to work with the connivance of the Prime Minister.

"Think," he said, "of what an advantage it would be to you to have daily information, from the fountain-head, of the Prime Minister's movements. The nights, for instance, when he was dining at home; the mornings when he would be working alone at his boxes."

Mr Smith saw the point. In spite of his conviction, in the first glow of pride over Rouen, that he alone had the imagination, the originality, to make full use of his doubleness, he had been increasingly bothered by the difficulty of knowing when it was, and when not, safe to play his little games. One can't have everything, and the prospect of daily contact with Downing Street was not unalluring. In the end he agreed to swap liberty for security, and the pact was made.

Littlejohn went straight to The Towers, and reported his success to his Chief. He was slightly chilled by his reception, for the Prime Minister had suffered too much from his *alter ego* to feel enthusiastic about owning him, even on a lead. He would have been happier to hear that the fellow had been accidentally drowned. But there was no alternative to ratifying the compact, and he managed to thank Littlejohn for his pains.

During the next two years the Prime Minister, from being a somewhat aloof and austere figure, respected from afar for his eloquence and abilities but attracting little warmth from a public who seldom saw him, was changed, by the joint efforts of Mr Smith and his Private Secretaries, into the "good old Andy" (and even "Andy Boy") whom the people grew to love. His frequent appearances at Cup Ties, at dog-races, at Big Fights, at Test Matches, not in Presidents' boxes or front seats, but in the crowd, in the queues, against the rails, in front of the Tavern, his eyes fixed upon the arena (lest they should meet other eyes known to them), his clothes old and comfortable, at times with a pipe (which he loathed) in his mouth—all these were faithfully recorded by his photographer for the pleasure of several million readers of the next morning's popular newspapers. People delighted to see him, in an old Panama hat and a dinghy, sculling himself, on the Phyllis Court side but in view of the Enclosure, at Henley. They were enraptured to catch a glimpse of him on a high box-seat and with a tiller in his hand, steering a 1900 Lanchester in the annual race of veteran cars to Brighton. They were deeply moved to see him stand, with bowed head, and in the rain, by the grave of a Welsh miner who had vilified him in the House of Commons for a decade. They smiled over his talks with little children in St James's Park. They shivered over his early dips, on November mornings, in the Serpentine. They laughed over his backchats with gypsy-women on Epsom heath. They devoutly hoped that the patient angler, in macintosh and sou'wester, at the end of Southend Pier, was catching fish. They admired the knowing look with which the Great Statesman surveyed fat cattle at agricultural shows. They laughed with him laughing, in a back seat at the Victoria Palace, at the antics of the Crazy Gang.

In the early days of this patient build-up the Prime Minister was inclined to be irritable at his secretaries' demands upon him. It was no fun to be asked to stay indoors all day in order that his double might attend a funeral or a Royal Show many hundred miles from London. But popularity is sweet to a politician, and the more he read about "Good old Andy" the better he liked it. There came a time when he began to make suggestions, to throw out ideas, to volunteer deprivations and sacrifices for the sake of "Andy Boy." In the end his collaboration was whole-hearted and enthusiastic.

"I really don't know," he remarked to Littlejohn, "how my predecessors got on without doubles."

When at length, still undefeated at the polls, he decided to make way for a younger man and to go to the Lords as Earl Smith of Portobello, the Prime Minister insisted on a farewell meeting with his faithful double. Downing Street was held to be too risky a rendezvous, and Mr Andrew Smith, to his pride and delight, entertained the great man and his secretaries in his Bayswater flat. Such was the force of habit, that only after the tame photographer had taken a flashlight picture of the reunion did they remember how private an occasion it must be. Even the photographer understood why the negative had to be extracted and destroyed in the presence of them all.

On the following day, Mr Andrew Smith, having promised to grow a massive and permanent beard, travelled back in moustache and dark glasses, to the Isle of Man. Hardened to deceit, he told his housekeeper with a straight face that he was at a loss to explain why no letter had reached him at Tokyo. And he alone of the conspirators did not feel that the award of the M.B.E. in the next Honours List, to Mr A. Smith "for public and political services" was grossly inadequate. For he had proved his point, he had done his bit for his country, and he had hugely enjoyed himself.

"Foot-slogger"

On a blazing day in late August 1914 the XXV*th* Hussars were being transported from Newhaven to Boulogne. The sea was calm, but below decks, where makeshift stables had been contrived, the heat was stifling, and, with one exception, the stable-guards alone, frequently relieved, were in attendance upon the uneasy, fidgeting horses. The exception was Private Simmons who, seemingly impervious to the stagnant, ammoniac atmosphere, stood or crouched by his horse's head almost throughout the crossing. His object was to soothe and comfort the disconcerted animal; his method was to talk to it, in his light sing-song Norfolk tones, about the good times they had had together, about the even better times to be hoped for in France. Oats, hay and linseed were mentioned in turn, but water was the topic that recurred most often—water at its coolest and most shining.

Private Simmons had been two years in the cavalry when war broke out. The son of a greengrocer in a small Norfolk town, he had been destined to succeed his father in the business. But from his earliest conscious years horses had been his passion, and carrots alone among vegetables had ever interested him. So his father sensibly apprenticed him, on leaving the village school at fourteen, to the proprietor of a livery-stable in Norwich. Mr Sewter, his employer, had taken pains with the boy and had taught him to ride, as well as all the intricacies of horse-management. When he was eighteen young Simmons, fired by the appearance of the horses of a cavalry regiment

26

then stationed at Norwich, had enlisted. And now he found himself, three weeks after the outbreak of war, a unit, important only to himself and to his mount, of the spearhead of the British Expeditionary Force.

Among his fellow-privates Simmons was not of much account. Above an unimpressive body, small and somewhat bandy-legged, his narrow face had the humourlessness of so many fanatical horse-lovers, for horses never make or see jokes. By the N.C.O.s he was regarded as being "dumb," for his mind worked slowly; and while his horsemanship was of a high order, and his work in stables and at saddle-cleaning blameless, his reactions at drill were sluggish, and while he knew the difference between "right-wheel" and "left-wheel" it took him a few seconds to translate that knowledge into action. In barrack-rooms and at mess he had little conversation, caring nothing for football or girls. He had twice been in trouble for pinching linseed from the Q.M.'s store, cooking it in his mess-tin, and surreptitiously mixing it with "Sewter's" feed in order to promote the glossiness of that cherished animal's coat.

"Sewter" was Simmons's private name for his horse. He was not romantic, but like most of his sort he was nostalgic, and he had chosen the name in memory of past contentment at the livery-stable. Officially Sewter was *"No. 29 br.g."* and bore that number branded by the farrier on his off hind hoof. Like all cavalry horses at the beginning of the first Great War, he was an animal of class, but being brown among bays, he needed all his rider's care in tail-pulling, banging and extra grooming, to hold his own for looks among his brighter companions. The need for solacing Sewter during the sea-passage had prevented Simmons from giving any attention to his personal situation, as one of the vanguard of an army sailing to war. And on arrival at Boulogne, with all the bustle of disembarking animals now as reluctant to leave the ship as they had been to board it, it was not until he found himself riding in half-section through the cobbled streets with cheering groups of Froggies pressing upon the very horses' flanks, throwing flowers and offering red

wine in thick glasses, that Private Simmons became fully conscious of what he was at. These people were making a fuss of
him because he had come to fight for them. Very well, he would
do his best for them. It was the first specifically soldier-like
thought that had come into Simmons's head since he had enlisted. But once lodged there, it remained with him for the
duration. As the squadron marched, at the walk, up the hill to
the transit-camp his troop sang:

> "All the birds of the air were a-sighin' and a-sobbin'
> When they heard of the death of poor Cock-Robin"

but, once arrived at the horse-lines, it was all watering and feeding and grooming and saddle-cleaning until the sun had set
over an incarnadined sea and Simmons was free to stumble,
his mess-tin full of stew, to the bell-tent he shared with seven
others. Tired as he was, he scribbled a pencil note to his Mum
before he slept. He dated it "Somewhere in France" and informed his Mum that where he was was not a patch on Blighty
but that he was in the pink and her loving son. Then Private
Simmons slept.

During the journey to railhead and the subsequent marches
of the next four days it was difficult for Private Simmons to
realise that he was going to war. The August sheaves, neck-to-
neck in the heavy-headed shocks; the apples beginning to turn
on the lime-washed trees; the wide unhedged fields; the poppies
and corncockles lining the dusty roads; the great white
poplars bedevilled with mistletoe; their Lombardy cousins that
appeared to stand at attention as the squadrons clopped and
jingled through their shadows: all these pleasant sights, de-
ployed beneath a burning sun, belied the cold truth that Private
Simmons was approaching, alternately at the walk and the
trot, a powerful and ruthless enemy between whom and himself
the guardian sea no longer rolled.

"Nice country," said the Major, at the squadron's head.

"Very," said his second-in-command, for they were both

country-lovers and deeply moved by the peace and beauty of
the scene.

But the Major's unwonted loquacity was not solely provoked
by the landscape. He was also in high feather because his command, "A" Squadron, had been detailed as "contact-squadron,"
which meant that it was being sent out into the blue ahead of
the Brigade to which his regiment belonged, in order to make
first contact with the enemy, and to discover what it could of
his numbers and intentions. To achieve this, the Squadron-
leader, having halted his four troops in a position which
afforded as much concealment as was available, detached a
number of patrols, each consisting of a junior officer or sergeant
and eight men, who rode out to reconnoitre the country in the
general direction of the advancing Germans. Their task was
twofold: to obtain information, and to prevent the enemy from
obtaining it. To achieve this second objective, the patrols were
ordered, should they discover an enemy patrol, to attack and
drive it back, preferably with the *"arme blanche."* For although
the cavalry carried rifles, slung across their shoulders with the
butts resting in leather buckets attached to the saddle, it was
upon his sword that a Hussar, in those early days, expected,
and intended, to rely. Upon his sword, and upon the combined
weight of his horse and himself behind that sword. There
might be cutting and thrusting in the mêlée after the charge;
but the deadly, the terrifying moment to those being charged
was the onslaught of horse, man and steel in rigid, unyielding
combination.

No enemy scouts or patrols had yet been encountered when
it was Private Simmons's turn to be detailed for patrol duty. He
rode out at dawn, in a heavy dew, under command of his
troop-sergeant, red-headed Sergeant Hall, with seven others
of his troop. A corporal and a private rode ahead, warily
using such cover as they could, the private keeping a station
from which he could see both the corporal leading and the
patrol following him. The country was undulating, with a scat-
tering of copses, belts and thickets to afford good means of

observing without being observed. In the open, mostly un-hedged fields, stooks stood in rows; here and there were stretches of unreaped corn. The larks were up and singing; a thin mist on the bottoms betokened another blazing day.

The patrol moved in single file, a horse's length apart. Private Simmons was the rear man; the fact that Sergeant Hall's familiar, slightly nagging voice was never once heard, not even when the ring of a shoe upon a stone caused him to turn his head in swift reproach, did give Simmons a feeling of strangeness and suspense; but even now his matter-of-fact mind did not quite take in that the little party were abroad, this lovely morning, to kill or to be killed. He was more con-cerned about the flies that were beginning to bother Sewter.

And then it happened. The patrol was moving through a thinly planted belt of oak and hazel when the soldier acting as connecting-link between itself and the corporal out ahead came into view at the further edge of the trees. His horse was turned about, facing the patrol, and his arm was raised above his head. It was the signal that game was afoot.

The patrol closed up to him at the trot. Sergeant Hall, in a whisper, ordered them to stay among the trees, then trotted forward to where the corporal was standing, dismounted, his field-glasses up to his eyes. In a couple of minutes the sergeant cantered back to his men. His small blue eyes glinted; his red moustache seemed to bristle.

"Oolans," he whispered.."We'll charge 'em. Form line when I give the signal and remember, a steady 'and-gallop and no racing. Knee to knee. Draw swords."

The patrol emerged from the belt and trotted, still in single file but closed up, head to tail, to where the corporal sat waiting, now remounted. He had withdrawn about thirty yards from the spot whence he and the sergeant had been observing, and he, too, had drawn his sword. The whole patrol was now united, concealed from the northern half of the visible landscape by one of these thickets of elder which grow round the edges of a disused marl-pit. On the other side of the pit was an old waggon-truck alongside a disjointed hedge of hawthorn bordering a stubble-field. About two hundred yards from the hedge, among a group of standing shocks, the corporal and sergeant had seen a patrol of German cavalry, most of them dismounted and with rifles in their hands, stalking, heads bent, from shock to shock.

The sergeant now explained to his men in a whisper that he proposed to lead them round the marl-pit in half-sections, cross a gap in the hedge and then immediately form line and charge across the open stubble.

"Understood?"

All nodded. Without another word the sergeant led off, curving round the east side of the marl-pit at a sharp trot. As they went, they heard the crack of rifles from the direction of the German patrol. The fire could not be directed at themselves, screened as they were by the elder-covered banks of the marl-pit. The enemy were clearly engaged with some other target, presumably one of their own patrols on an adjoining sector. Nothing, thought the sergeant, could be better. He might well find himself charging them from behind.

But to Private Simmons the report of those rifle-shots had quite another significance. Slow-minded as he was, they shocked him into one of the quickest decisions of his life. In the short time that it took the little cavalcade to swing round the curve of the marl-pit and turn left-handed, through the first gap in the hedge, on to the stubble, he decided what to do. As he rode up into his place at the right of the line, he disengaged the butt of his slung rifle from its bucket, slipped off his horse on the near side, let go of his reins, and, as the horse on his left broke into a canter, seized, with his left hand, the stirrup-leather of its rider. As the little line began their charge, knee to knee, bodies bent forward and swords held rigidly at the full extent of their arms, a small, bandy-legged soldier, much encumbered by a rifle which banged about at his back, was running and leaping in line with them, holding on, for dear life, to his neighbour's stirrup-leather with his left hand, and attempting, unsuccessfully, to keep his sword pointed forwards with his right. It could not last long. Private Simmons's neighbour, who alone had seen him dismount, had no mind, if he could help it, to lose his alignment by dragging a foot-soldier with him in his first charge. Swearing like the trooper that he was, he kicked his spurred heel into Private Simmons's left wrist with a violence that compelled the little runner to let go. The seven swept on, straight towards the stooks, and Private Simmons, who was no runner, followed them, panting and blowing, his left hand gripping his sling to prevent his rifle from belabouring him, his right arm aching from his efforts to carry his sword in an aggressive and hostile position. And he could hardly restrain his sobs—sobs not of vexation for his own plight, but of anxiety for Sewter. For Sewter, relieved of the weight upon his back, had joined in the charge, easily outstripping the rest and, although now masked from Simmons's sight by the mounted horses, must have been the first to reach the enemy.

As to them, the sergeant had been right. Intent on firing, from such concealment as the stooks afforded, upon a distant British patrol, they had lost their heads when, turning to the rattle and thud of the charge upon their rear, they had seen, swift and compact, the oncoming line of steel. One or two fired ill-aimed shots as they rose from their stooks, but most instinctively made for the bunch of led horses in a little hollow to one flank. Scattered as they were, only one was borne down by the charging patrol; the rest, unable to make the distance to their horses, held up their hands. The two horse-holders galloped away, leaving their charges to canter, snorting, round the field. And the victors were so busy collecting the dismounted prisoners and pursuing the loose horses, that not one of them noticed the arrival in their midst of Private Simmons.

Simmons had good eyes. Exhausted as he was, he had noticed, from his vantage-point at ground-level, that a fallen stook on the extreme left of the miniature field of battle was shaking its golden locks of, seemingly, its own volition. "The b——," thought Simmons. He made straight for the stook, straddled it with his bandy legs, and perceived, immediately beneath him, a small portion of grey uniform very tightly stretched over a Teutonic behind. He was not the man to deal cruelly with a recumbent enemy. But the invitation was too tempting to be altogether refused, and Private Simmons jabbed. There was a yell which made the sergeant turn his head, to see a large German, half-draped in sheaves, kneeling with his hands up, at the feet of the little Hussar.

"Good boy," said the sergeant. "Bring him along."

Simmons brought him along, at the sword's point, but the sergeant's approval was short-lived. Private Figgis, who had ridden on Simmons's left hand, and was still rabid at the little man's conduct in hanging on to his horse, had by now asked for a private word in the ear of Sergeant Hall. And when the patrol-leader had heard the story of a man deliberately dismounting and letting go his horse when preparing to charge, he was shocked to the core.

"Here, you!" he shouted. "What's all this? You're a disgrace to the British Army. Consider yourself under arrest. You're for it, my lad. What you do it for?"

"It was the shootin', Sergeant," said Simmons. "When I hard them there Garmans a-shootin'——"

Sergeant Hall turned purple. "Gawd help us!" he said. "And you a Hussar! 'Ere!" he turned to Private Figgis, "take 'is sword and rifle—no, 'e can carry that—take 'is sword and ammunition. And you, Simmons, you'll ride 'ome with the prisoners. Where's your bloody 'orse?"

As it happened Simmons's bloody horse, Sewter, after an enjoyable canter round the field with a couple of German horses against whom he appeared to have no ill-will, had now quietly walked back to his little rider. Simmons took the bridle and looked him over with concern.

"He haven't come to no harm," he said.

But the sergeant was now speechless with shame. His triumph had turned to dust. As he rode back at the head of the victorious patrol, now escorting in its midst five German prisoners and Private Simmons, he wondered what charge to bring against the man. "It was the shootin', Sergeant." Must he call it cowardice in the face of the enemy? That meant death, and eternal disgrace to the Regiment. And after all, the little soldier had turned up, although late and on foot, at the scene of the fray. He had even bagged a prisoner through his quick, attentive eye. The sergeant gave it up. He must report the facts and leave the Squadron-leader to formulate a suitable charge.

In due course the party arrived at the wooded hollow where the squadron was bivouacking. The Squadron-leader was a stern enforcer of the adage that troops in reserve, when not eating, should be sleeping. Hence only the men on guard and the Major himself, busy at a folding table under a tree, were stirring. The Major, seeing the live prisoners—the most valuable of all captures—came forward himself to congratulate the patrol and to hear its leader's report. The men were led off by the corporal to water the horses at a nearby stream and so to the horse-lines. The prisoners were put under guard; and the sergeant went with the Squadron-leader to his table, there to make a fuller report and to take his orders for sending the prisoners back to Brigade H.Q. for interrogation. All this took time. Then came dinner, the sleeping men having been roused for their alternate duty of eating; and after dinner a second patrol rejoined, the one that had been fired at, without casualties, by the defeated Germans. Fresh patrols had to be detailed, briefed, and despatched; reports written to H.Q.; maps consulted and marked; guards and outpost relieved; and the shadows of the encircling trees were beginning to lengthen before the sergeant had a breathing-space in which to report to the Squadron-leader that he had a man under arrest.

"What for?"

"I can't rightly say, sir, never 'aving 'eard of such a thing in all my life," and he recounted the events of the morning.

"Queer," said the Major. "Bring the man here. Any witnesses?"

"Only Private Figgis, sir."

"Bring them both."

A few minutes later Private Simmons was standing at attention, cap off, in front of the camp-table. Private Figgis stood, cap on head, at one side of the table, Sergeant Hall at the other. Private Figgis, still resentful, described how the prisoner had deliberately dismounted, abandoned his horse, and attempted to assist, as the French would say, in the charge as a hanger-on.

"But I wouldn't 'ave none of that," said Private Figgis.

It was the first time Sergeant Hall had heard this part of the story, and he felt glad that he had not made a charge of "cowardice." At least Private Simmons had himself been prepared to face the shooting.

"What do you say to all this, Simmons?"

"Well, sir, when I hard them there Garmans a-shootin' I thought to meself as how that wasn't hardla fair to a hoss to ax him to risk hisself where I shouldn't hev no power to look arter him."

"A war-horse must go to war," said the Major.

"But he look to his roider to take care on him. If them there Garmans had a-used their swords, same as us, I'd a-rid Sewter at 'em and welcome, cause I reckon to ha' got them afore they got him."

"But you knew that all cavalry carry rifles nowadays. You carry one yourself."

"That's roight, sir. But in trainin' back hoom we allus put our hosses on one soide afore we start a'shootin', sir. So when I hard them rifles goin' off, I thought to meself, well if that's the game I better tarn the old hoss loose."

"I should have thought you knew enough about horses, Simmons, to be sure that yours would follow the others? Did you expect him to go and hide behind a hedge on his own?"

"Well, that warn't vera loikely, perhaps. But if he choose to goo a-chargin' as a woluntair, there wasn't nawthin' I cud dew, were there? On'y I didn't see my way to make a dumb animal goo where I cudn't look arter him."

35

"So you've told us before."

The Squadron-leader doodled for a few moments on a message-form.

"I don't think you intended to commit a military crime, Simmons," he said. "But in future you will put your country before your horse. Is that clear?"

Simmons's jaw fell. He looked dumbfounded.

"Lawks, Major, I never thought o' that!"

"But you will."

"I'll troy."

"You'd better."

In that night's squadron orders Private Simmons was detailed as groom to the Squadron-leader. In the days to come the regiment was more often upon its feet than mounted: at Ypres, in the chalk trenches near Vermelles, in the mud and slime of La Bassée, while their swords remained in their scabbards. Private Simmons, as an officer's groom, did far less walking than his fellows. But the story of his solitary dismounted charge got about, and for the rest of the war he was known in the regiment as "Foot-slogger."

A Writ for Libel

THE atmosphere in the senior partner's room of Raynham and Ryburgh, respectable solicitors of Lincoln's Inn Fields, on a morning of early June in the year 1959, was more than strained; it was painful. The usually placid brow of Mr Raynham, the senior partner, was clouded: he hated unpleasantness. Beyond his wide, all but unencumbered knee-hole desk there sat, in two straight-backed leather-covered armchairs, the stout despondent figure of his esteemed client Mr Bagthorpe, head of the publishing firm of Bagthorpe & Harpley, and the slim, indignant one of Mr Paul Runton, that firm's latest, twenty-four-year-old author. A little to one side, on an armless chair suited to his station in life, sat Mr Croft, Mr Raynham's managing clerk.

Had the eminent publisher and his youthful author been able to afford a moment's relaxation in which to raise their eyes to the high Queen Anne window and to the tree-tops beyond, the joyful air of the still adolescent foliage reflecting the June sunlight might have reminded them of their own festive mood but a few days since. For Paul Runton's first novel, *Under the Counter,* had been received by the critics with unanimous approval, and while commendatory cuttings came flowing into, a most satisfactory number of copies had been flowing out of, his publisher's office. But they were not able to afford it. They had been listening to Mr Croft, and Mr Croft's tale had been, for both of them, a knock-down blow.

Three days earlier, publisher and author (as well as a firm of printers in Edinburgh) had been served by a highly reputable firm of solicitors acting for a Mr Stogumber Pank of Brecon Walk, Chelsea, with writs for libel. Their first reaction was one of amusement. This must be an elaborate joke by one of Paul's friends, provoked by the outlandish name chosen by Paul, who had been a Dickensian since boyhood, for one of his minor but most villainous characters. But a telephone conversation between Mr Bagthorpe and the reputable solicitors acting for the imaginary Mr Pank had been alarming. The lawyers informed the publishers, stiffly enough, that they had taken steps to satisfy themselves that, improbable as was his name, their client did indeed keep a shop in Brecon Walk, and that the description of him, his beard, his spectacles and his shop, detailed and particular as the young disciple of Dickens had made it, corresponded in all respects with the facts. They referred Mr Bagthorpe to his author, as briefly and sternly as a bank refers a stumer cheque to its drawer.

The interview between publisher and author had been stormy. Mr Bagthorpe reproached the young man bitterly for having taken this queer name from a shop-front (as is reputed to have been Dickens's habit).

"I tell you I invented it. I took Stogumber from Shaw and Pank for the jolt of it."

"But you made your Stogumber Pank keep a shop 'in one of those small streets leading out of the King's Road'—just where he does live."

"I've never been down any of them. I hardly know Chelsea. It's a pure coincidence."

"An expensive one for you, Runton. I must remind you of Clause 3 of our agreement."

"But I *haven't* libelled anybody! I shall fight this to the last."

"Who'll believe you?"

"Mr Bagthorpe, are you calling me a liar?"

Mr Bagthorpe, who had hitherto been much impressed with his youthful author's candid and ingenuous ways, looked straight into Paul's eyes and faltered. Paul must, he felt sure, be a liar; but he would prefer to have it said, in such round terms, by someone else.

"We had better see Raynham," he said, temporarily quelled.

Within a couple of hours they did see Raynham. That experienced solicitor, who avoided Paul's eyes as far as possible and addressed himself throughout to Mr Bagthorpe, called it an "unfortunate affair," but said that since so far they had only a report of a report to go upon, he would prefer, before advising them, to make his own investigations. He invited them to return the next morning, and sent "our Mr Croft" to Chelsea to see for himself.

The gist of what "our Mr Croft" had finished describing at the moment this story opens can be told shortly enough. At the end of Brecon Walk farthest from the King's Road he had found a small shop, with a single window on the right side of the door. It appeared to stock newspapers and magazines, boiled sweets, cheap stationery, birthday cards, infantile picture-books and the like. Over the window was painted: STOGUMBER PANK. At the side of the door hung a birdcage containing a greenish canary. Mr Croft had entered the shop and bought sevenpennyworth of sweets. He had been served by a thin, youngish, spectacled man with a sparse bristly beard and an unexpectedly cultivated accent. There was a closed door at the rear of the little shop. When Mr Croft had finished his tale Mr Raynham opened the copy of *Under the Counter* which lay before him at a page already marked by a paper slip. And otiosely, as far as his two clients, who knew the wretched passage by heart, were concerned, but perhaps to give himself a further short reprieve from the distasteful but unavoidable moment of decision, he read aloud in a flat, disinterested tone, a few salient phrases from Paul's description of the humble shop in Chelsea in which his Stogumber Pank carried on his nefarious practices. For Paul's Stogumber was a receiver of stolen goods, a blackmailer, a pimp, a harbourer of crooks, and only too cowardly to be a murderer as well. And although Mr Raynham skipped—with a murmur of er-er-er, the loving, almost

Balzacian care with which Paul had catalogued the trashy articles dealt in by Pank, and the pretty passage describing the soft pizzicato sounds made by the canary as he hopped from perch to perch, there had been nothing in Mr Croft's narrative of which the exact counterpart was not to be found in Paul's.

Mr Raynham stopped reading and looked at Mr Bagthorpe.

"You will have to settle," he said, "and I'm afraid it won't be cheap. But he may take less than a jury would give him."

"Of course we must settle," said Bagthorpe, without glancing at Paul. "What amount would you propose?"

"Pank seems to be in humble circumstances," said Mr Raynham. "Five thousand pounds might seem a lot of money to him."

Bagthorpe swung round to face Paul.

"What do you say, Runton? I have recourse to you, as you know."

Paul stood up, almost too furious to find utterance.

"I haven't libelled anybody," he shouted. "I made up the whole thing—and I'm not going to pay a penny!"

"That, Mr Runton, is, if you refuse to settle, for a jury to say," said the solicitor, "and they might well make it ten thousand pounds or even more."

Paul picked up his hat and stick, which trembled in his hand.

"I've done with you both," he said. "I will *not* be called a liar!" And he strode, not without dignity, to the door, with which he felt angry, too, as he descended the stairs, for it had been too heavy to bang.

Enraged, and even more confounded by his predicament, Paul walked rapidly westward, receiving an occasional stab of pain as he passed the windows of bookshops in which copies of *Under the Counter* were displayed in batches of half-a-dozen or more. With what kindness, with what personal interest his dear Mr Bagthorpe had concerned himself even with the design of that beguiling dust-cover! How paternally he had shared in Paul's triumphant excitement when those early glowing reviews had appeared! And now, at the first menace of a storm, the old humbug was flying to cover and accusing him, his cherished young author, of cold and calculated dishonesty! It was not to be borne. Had Paul realised that in a couple of days not a copy of his novel would be found even on the back shelves of a single bookshop, his exasperation would have been even more frantic.

Paul's knowledge of the law of libel was vague. But he could not believe that any English law could penalise the innocent. He admitted to himself that the facts were extraordinary, and on the face of them inexplicable. None the less, old Raynham had allowed himself to be terrorised by the facts against Paul and had given no weight at all to just as palpable a fact on the other side: his innocence. The thought so infuriated him that he walked several hundred yards beyond his next turning. The necessity of retracing his steps for those several hundred yards calmed him: after all, he reflected, Raynham was not infallible. There must be other lawyers. Men who would be for, not against, their client. It was then that he remembered meeting, at a small dinner-party, a youngish solicitor called Mainwaring, with whom he had had an agreeable talk. The lawyer had struck Paul as having quality, and an open-minded attitude to things generally. Paul even remembered about him that he was a junior partner in the firm of Doughton and Toftrees, of Southampton Row.

A telephone-book gave him the address, a telephone-box the voice, of Charles Mainwaring, who remembered Paul perfectly. If it was really so urgent, let him come at six that evening. Paul did so, and found Mainwaring, who was only a junior partner, in a smaller and shabbier, but less intimidating, room than Mr Raynham's. It was both more and less like a lawyer's room; more in having black, japanned boxes, with names in white paint upon their sides, stacked against the walls, and less in having a jug of flowers upon the table and golf-clubs in a corner. Mainwaring himself, as before at the dinner-party, once again impressed Paul as a man at whom you would look twice in any company.

"Congratulations on your book," he said to Paul, as he re-seated himself after drawing up a chair for his client.

"I'm afraid condolences would be more appropriate," said Paul. "It's my book I've come to see you about." He took the book from under his arm and leant forward to hand it to the solicitor, then told him, at length, of his predicament.

"I'm completely baffled," he concluded. Mainwaring did not evade Paul's gaze. He looked him straight in the eyes and, with no hint of suspicion in his tone but rather one of compassion for a young man in trouble, said: "You certainly are up against it. You must give me time to think this over. I will call you tomorrow or the day after." After taking down Paul's telephone number, and the address of the house in Bayswater where Paul lived, as aloofly as befits a coming young writer, with his parents, Mainwaring shook his hand with a reassuring warmth. At least, Paul felt, as he walked homeward, he had found an adviser who would assume his truthfulness until it had been disproved.

Mainwaring, left alone, began his meditations on the case. He read and re-read the pertinent passages in the novel with care. He then leant back in his chair, drove his fingers through his hair, and began to polish the bowl of his pipe by rubbing it slowly up and down the side of his nose.

Mainwaring was accustomed, very sensibly, not to let himself be bemused by such a word as "inexplicable," since everything can be explained. Nor did he, like Mr Raynham, allow himself to be terrorised, as Paul had put it, by one set of facts until a possible, however improbable, alternative set of facts had been duly weighed. As a result of a prolonged meditation and pipe-polishing, a highly improbable, but not impossible, solution of the puzzle did present itself to his mind. He decided to take the next day off and to see things for himself.

At about ten o'clock the next morning Mainwaring, in a very old suit and a discoloured hat, passed and re-passed the unpretentious little shop in Brecon Walk. He had rather hoped to catch the eye of the owner, but, small as the place was, he could not make out whether the shadowed and shallow space behind the counter was occupied. So, after chirping ingratiatingly to an unresponsive green canary, he pushed open the door and went in. An old-fashioned door-bell tinkled and as the lanky, spectacled young man with a beard came from the inner room, Mainwaring had a glimpse of a fly-blown print of Lord Nelson hanging on the dotted wallpaper, and of a ginger cat curled up on a kitchen chair.

"Mr Pank?" he asked, removing his hat to show that he was no mere customer.

"Yes," said the young man. "I'm Pank. Anything I can do for you?"

"It's just a shot in the dark, of course," said Mainwaring, "but I've been hunting for a shop in these parts and as yours is the sort of thing I'm looking for, I thought there'd be no harm in asking whether you would care to do a deal?"

"Well, I'm not the owner," said Pank. "I've only got a lease. But as it happens, it runs out at the end of September, and I'm not renewing. If you can wait till then I daresay my landlord would re-let or even sell."

"Business not good enough?" Mainwaring spoke sharply with a touch of suspicion.

"There's a living in it," said Pank, "but I want to get into the country."

"I suppose I could wait," said Mainwaring uncertainly. "Could you let me have the landlord's name and address?"

"It's his agents, Keyes and Flatt, that you'll have to see," said Pank. "I got the place through them and pay them the rent and so on."

"Would you mind writing that down for me?" said Mainwaring. "I've a head like a sieve."

Pank went into the back room for a piece of paper and Mainwaring followed him in far enough to see a framed photograph of King Edward VII in a white nautical cap, standing with Sir Thomas Lipton on the deck of a yacht, hung upon the wall opposite to the print of Lord Nelson.

Pank scribbled "Keyes and Flatt, 181A Cromwell Road" on a half-sheet of paper in a bold individual hand. "Mr Green's the man to ask for," he said.

Mainwaring took the paper and thanked him warmly. "You don't live over the shop, do you?" he asked.

Pank shook his head.

"There's only what you see here. But you have the right to use the lavatory on the first floor."

"Well, good-bye, and many thanks again."

"Don't mention it."

Mainwaring went at once to the Cromwell Road. His visit to Mr Green was fruitful, but led to a further expedition to a house near Notting Hill Gate, which also proved profitable. Returning to his office on the top of a bus he found himself, to his surprise, whistling "Lillibullero." A girl looked round, and he stopped. But in no time he was humming the "Ride of the Valkyries" under his breath. All the same, when he set the chain of facts so far verified against those which had so forcibly floored Mr Raynham, there was a link still missing, a link which Runton alone could supply.

By five o'clock Paul was again in Mainwaring's office.

"I've had a good day so far," said Mainwaring. "But before I tell you about it I want you to answer a few questions."

The questions and answers went swimmingly enough, and a clue to the missing link was found. But to discover a possible link is one thing; to establish it as proved in a court of law is quite another. And although Mainwaring could see a slender chance of conclusive corroboration, his young client's memory failed him at the critical point.

"But surely you can remember whether it was a neat parcel?"

Mainwaring's features were tense with the effort of willing Paul to recollect.

"It must have meant a lot to you; surely you can see yourself cutting the string?"

Paul laughed. "I expect my mama untied it," he said. "We

were all at breakfast, you see. And she has a thing about string —she can't bear to see it wasted."

"Nor the wrapping-paper either?"

"I expect so. But honestly I don't remember."

"Ring up your lady mother now," said Mainwaring, "and ask when she can receive us."

Mrs Runton was at home, and solicitor and client took a taxi to Bayswater.

Napoleon wanted his generals to be lucky: had Mainwaring been one of them he might have won his marshal's baton then and there. For it turned out that not only did Mrs Runton hoard string but, if the parcel were neat enough, the wrapping-paper as well. A diligent search in a hall-cupboard discovered a smoothed-out sheet of brown paper addressed to Paul, and bearing a postmark dated in the previous December. The conjectured missing link was now a solid corroborated fact.

Mainwaring rewarded Paul's co-operative parent with a full account of his day's work.

"We could compel our Stogumber to withdraw the writ, of course," said Mainwaring, "but that would be too kind to him and to your friends Bagthorpe and Raynham. My advice to you is to defend the action in open court. I will try to get hold of counsel tomorrow. I know the very man if he's available." Paul was delighted.

Next morning *The Times* contained a formal statement by Messrs Bagthorpe & Harpley, Publishers, offering a full and frank apology to Mr Stogumber Pank of Chelsea for a serious libel contained in Mr Paul Runton's book *Under the Counter*. It added that substantial compensation had been paid to Mr Pank and that all unsold copies had been withdrawn from the bookshops and libraries. Paul also received a letter from Raynham and Ryburgh calling upon him to indemnify his publishers under Clause 3 of his contract in the sum of five thousand pounds plus costs incurred. He handed it to Mainwaring, whose reply, in terms as near to impoliteness as is admissible between members of the Law Society, told that eminent firm where they got off. (They retaliated with a writ.) And on the following day Mr Wood-Dalling, a rising junior consulted by Mr Mainwaring, accepted a brief to appear for Paul with that rubbing of hands with which rising lawyers habitually express pleasure.

During the months that must intervene between the serving of a writ and the trial of an action, there was a good deal of pleasurable gossip about the affair in publishing and literary circles, for cases where a publisher apologises, pays heavy damages and withdraws a book from circulation, while the author stands pat and decides to fight the action, are rare enough. And when at length the day came for the case to be tried, the public seats in Mr Justice Pinkney's court were packed.

Peeping cautiously from a corner of the gallery, as if half-ashamed to be discovered at a scene to which it could only have come to gloat over a once cherished client, was the large pink face of Mr Bagthorpe. Beside it was the still larger grey countenance of Mr Raynham.

Mr Justice Pinkney had the appearance less of a judge than of a fox-terrier. Eager, watchful, alert, with a sharp little up-turned nose, his Lordship lacked only a pair of cocked ears to make the resemblance complete. It was clear that he loved his job.

In opening the plaintiff's case to the jury, counsel for Stogumber Pank could not, he said, find words in which to describe the cruelty, the malice, the downright wickedness of the defendant's conduct, although to Paul he seemed to have discovered plenty. What made the libel so particularly atrocious, counsel told the jury, was the malignant care taken by the defendant through the piling of detail upon detail, all of them accurate to a hair, to leave no possible doubt in the minds of Mr Pank's friends and neighbours, the whole of Chelsea and the world in general, that Mr Stogumber Pank and none other, was the receiver, the blackmailer, the pimp

46

and the coward described in the defendant's pages. Counsel proceeded to read aloud the offending passages and said that he would call witnesses to prove that every smallest item, "down to his canary and his cat," of the novel's account of the plaintiff and his surroundings was true to life. He contrasted the gentlemanly behaviour of the defendant's publishers, in immediately withdrawing the book and paying a large sum in damages, with the defendant's own callous, impudent and impertinent conduct in brazening it out in a court of law. How a reputable firm of lawyers could have permitted him to do so was beyond counsel's comprehension. And they had pleaded neither justification nor fair comment—merely a general denial that the words complained of were libellous! In all his experience he had never heard of such a case, and he had no doubt that the jury, in assessing the damages for this outrage, would teach the defendant a lesson he would remember for the rest of his life.

The jury, consisting of ten men and two women, remained, as is the way of British juries, stolidly expressionless, but their eyes could be seen to be darting this way and that as they attempted to identify, on the benches reserved for the solicitors and their clients, a young man who could be guilty of such unprecedented wickedness. Most of them decided upon a lanky, spectacled, bearded young man whose unperturbed, even smug demeanour, must surely distinguish him as the brazen one. There was accordingly a look of surprise in their eyes when, counsel having called for Mr Stogumber Pank, this very young man rose and entered the witness-box.

Mr Pank gave his evidence quietly and clearly. His counsel took him over the whole ground, neglecting no detail of the exhaustive picture of himself and his shop drawn by the author of *Under the Counter*. Only when his evidence in chief was concluded, and Mr Wood-Dalling rose to cross-examine, did the plaintiff affect a rather appealing air of injured innocence.

Mr Wood-Dalling had every symptom of being as "rising"

as in fact he was. His chin was firm, his upper-lip long, his voice vibrant, his bearing assured, and he manipulated his eye-glasses with the forensic skill of a Carson. He looked first at the jury with an air of trust and benevolence; then stared hard at the plaintiff for a second or two before he spoke.

"Mr Pank, your real name is Peter Bale?"

"I trade as Stogumber Pank."

"I know you do. But I'm asking for your real name. Is it Peter Bale?"

"It is."

The plaintiff's counsel and solicitor could have been seen to exchange glances.

"And you lodge in Jamaica Row, Notting Hill, with Mrs Johnson?"

"I don't see what that has to do with this case."

"No, but I do. Do you lodge with Mrs Johnson?"

"I do."

"And did you see your landlady in the lobby outside this court this morning?"

"I did not."

"All the more pleasure for you when you see her in the witness-box. Why do you wear spectacles?"

"My sight is bad."

"When did it become bad?"

"I—er—I don't remember exactly. Quite a time ago."

"What do you mean by quite a time? A year or so?"

"About that, I should think."

"Will you be surprised to hear from Mrs Johnson that you wore no spectacles before January last?"

"She could be mistaken."

"We shall see. What oculist did you consult about your eyes?"

"I don't remember."

"But you must have consulted one?"

"I suppose so."

"In what part of London did he live?"

48

"I don't remember."

"Those spectacles of yours are rather unusual, aren't they?"

"In what way?"

"That band that goes over your nose. Isn't it unusually thick?"

"I shouldn't have thought so."

"Wasn't it made thick to hide a wart on the bridge of your nose?"

Counsel for the plaintiff rose to his feet.

"Me lud, I object. Must this witness be submitted to these irrelevant personalities?"

"I shall show, me lud, that the question is highly relevant to my case," said Mr Wood-Dalling.

"Very well. You must answer the question, Mr Bale," said the judge. Mr Wood-Dalling repeated his question. "Was it made thick to hide a wart on the bridge of your nose?"

"If you must know, yes."

"And there's another peculiarity about these spectacles, is there not?"

"I don't know what you mean."

"Well, the eye-pieces contain plain glass, don't they? There are no lenses in them."

"What good would they be to me if they were?"

"What indeed!" said Mr Wood-Dalling. "Would you mind passing them to the jury?"

The plaintiff looked appealingly at the judge.

"Must I, my Lord?"

"Do as counsel asks you," said the judge.

The plaintiff removed his spectacles, revealing an unsightly wart, of a deep purple colour, the sort of which it could be said "Once seen, never forgotten." An usher took the spectacles and handed them to the jury, who passed them round the jury-box, each member in turn taking a squint through them.

The usher was about to hand them back to the witness when the judge leant forward. "Give them to me, please," he said. The usher gave them to the Associate, who stood up to pass them up to the judge, who examined them briefly. "Plain glass," he said, and handed them down again. The witness, on finally regaining his spectacles, replaced them on his nose with a hand that trembled.

"Perhaps you remember now that you did *not* consult an oculist?" continued Mr Wood-Dalling with a glance at the jury. "But we will leave your plain-glass spectacles. When did you begin to grow a beard?"

"Some time last autumn, I think."

"Do you know a Mr Green of Keyes and Flatt Ltd, the house agents?"

"I do."

"Will it surprise you to hear from him, as well as from Mrs Johnson, when they give their evidence, that you had no beard before January last? No spectacles and no beard?"

"It's difficult to be certain about dates."

"But you remember visiting Mr Green at his office on January 1st to sign the lease for your shop in Brecon Walk?"

"I do."

"Was it your first venture as a shop-keeper?"

"It was."

"What was your previous occupation?"

"I am a writer."

"Had anything published?"

"Not so far."

"Why did you take the lease for only nine months?"

"I wanted to see how I liked shop-keeping."

"Are you going to renew the lease in September?"

"No."

"The shop will have served its purpose by then?"

"I don't know what you mean."

"I think you do. But never mind. Now tell me, Did you, on a day in December last, find a parcel left on the top of a bus?"

"Certainly not!" The reply came sharp as a pistol-shot. The plaintiff's solicitor and counsel shifted in their seats. In the gallery the pink face of Mr Bagthorpe turned towards the grey one of Mr Raynham.

"Why did my question startle you so?"

"I am not in the least startled."

"Wasn't it because you *did* find a parcel left on the top of a bus?"

"I tell you I did not."

"You who couldn't remember the name of your oculist or the date when you took to plain spectacles and began to grow a beard are positive about an insignificant incident that can hardly have made any impression on you?"

"Positive."

"Then let me jog your memory. Just look at this. Usher!" Mr Wood-Dalling drew from under the papers on the desk before him a piece of ordinary brown wrapping-paper and handed it to the usher, who carried it to the witness-box.

"Is not the handwriting on that brown paper yours?"

The plaintiff examined the paper, that shook a little in his hand.

"I wouldn't swear to it," he said.

"But surely you must know your own handwriting?"

"It varies so."

"It hasn't varied much between the script on that brown paper and the script on this white one, has it?" Mr Wood-Dalling held out to the usher the half-sheet of notepaper on which the plaintiff had written the address of Keyes and Flatt for Mainwaring. "You recognise that as your own, don't you? And you recognise, sitting here below me (counsel pointed at Mainwaring) the gentleman for whom you wrote it in your back room, don't you?"

"Let me see those pieces of paper," said the judge. They were duly handed up, the judge gave them a glance, and passed them down again. "Give them to the jury," he instructed the usher. The plaintiff did not at all like the way the jury looked at him after their inspection of the two pieces of paper. Besides, his nerve was going.

"Let me ask you again," said counsel. "The handwriting on both these pieces of paper is yours, is it not?"

"I suppose so."

"Why suppose? Is it or isn't it?"

"Yes, it is."

"And the address written by you on the brown paper is that of the defendant at his home in Bayswater?"

"It seems to be."

"You mean it is?"

"Yes."

"And the postmark on the brown paper is of some date, not decipherable, in December last?"

"I didn't look at the postmark."

"Please look now." The usher again took the brown paper to the witness.

"Well?"

"It seems to be."

"I think the ladies and gentlemen of the jury must by now realise that 'it seems to be' is your way of saying 'it is'." This got a smile from the jury which made the plaintiff's counsel and solicitor again exchange glances. Mr Wood-Dalling went on.

"So you agree you addressed a brown paper parcel to the defendant at his home on some day in December last?"

"I suppose I must have."

"What was in the parcel?"

"I can't tell you. I didn't look inside it."

"Is Mr Runton a friend of yours?"

"I never met him in my life."

"Are you telling the jury that you wrapped up an unknown something and posted it to a total stranger?"

"I didn't wrap it up. I found it and returned it to its owner."

"A few minutes ago you sharply denied that you had found it. Was that a lie told on oath?"

"I said I had not found it on a bus. And I didn't."

"I see. Where did you find it?"

"Lying in the road."

"Which road?"

"I really can't remember."

"And what did you do?"

"Picked it up and returned it to the owner."

"How was it wrapped up?"

"In this piece of brown paper."

"Look at that paper again, please. Is not the only writing on it the defendant's address in your own handwriting?"

The witness turned the paper over and over in his hand. "It looks like it."

"So how could you know the address of the owner?"

"I remember now. The parcel was so muddy I had to re-wrap it."

"But to unwrap it first?"

"I suppose so."

"And what did you find?"

"It felt like a book of sorts."

"So you only felt it. Were you able to 'feel' the owner's address?"

"It was written on an inside wrapping."

"What sort of wrapping?"

"Paper."

"But you looked inside that inner wrapping, didn't you?"

"I did not."

"So it will be a surprise to you to hear from the defendant and others, when they go into the box, that the only place where his name and address were written was on the corner of the typescript which the parcel contained?"

"That won't be correct."

"When you found the muddy parcel in the road, did you take it home with you?"

"No, to a post office."

"Where they gave you a nice clean piece of brown paper and string?"

"I suppose so."

"Let me suppose for once that you leave off supposing. Did they?"

"Yes."

"Where was the post office?"

"I really can't remember."

"I don't wonder. Now, Mr Bale, remember that you are on your oath. Did you not take that parcel home, or to some place where you could examine it at leisure, discover that it was the typescript of a novel called *Under the Counter* with the defendant's name on the corner, begin to read it, come across the Stogumber Pank passages, and conceive the brilliant idea that if you could contrive to be living the life of Stogumber at the time the novel was published—an event you, as a writer, had no difficulty in foreseeing—you would be in an unassailable position to win thumping damages from all concerned?"

The witness raised his voice for the first time. "It's not true!" he shouted.

"Then how do you explain, that, within three weeks or less of having this novel in your hands, you, as a writer, hired and stocked a small shop in Chelsea for nine months only, adopted the outlandish name of Stogumber Pank, procured a plain pair of glass spectacles adapted to conceal a too easily recognisable blemish, began to grow a beard, acquired a green canary and a sandy cat, as the novel demanded, and carefully surrounded yourself with every article described in the book?"

The witness shouted for the second time.

"I deny everything!"

Mr Wood-Dalling looked at the jury. "I have no more questions," he said, and sat down.

The judge looked towards plaintiff's counsel.

"I shall not re-examine, me lud," he said in a flat voice. "I shall call no more witnesses."

The judge turned and looked at Mr Wood-Dalling who again stood up.

"I shall waste no time in opening the defendant's case," he said. "I now call the defendant."

Paul left his seat at Mainwaring's side and entered the box. But the jury's heads had been already put together. They gave one look at Runton and resumed their whispering. Before counsel had got further than asking Paul his name and address the foreman of the jury was standing up, facing the judge.

"My lord," he said, "we have all heard enough of this case. May we return our verdict now?"

"Not unless the defence agrees," said the judge. "Mr Wood-Dalling?"

"We shall be content, me lud."

"What do you say, Mr Speke?"

Mr Speke stood up. "I can only say, me lud, that should this case go on, I shall not trouble to cross-examine my learned friend's witnesses."

The large pink and grey faces in the corner of the gallery disappeared from view.

"Very good," said the judge. He turned to the foreman of the jury. "You have heard what counsel have said. In these circumstances you may return your verdict now."

The Associate rose and formally asked the jury for their verdict.

"We find for the defendant," said the foreman, "and that is the verdict of us all."

The judge no longer looked like a fox-terrier. He looked like a judge. He said,

"Judgement for the defendant with costs. And I direct that all the papers in this case, including the shorthand report of the evidence, be impounded and sent to the Public Prosecutor."

On that the Court rose.

An hour later Paul and his parents were sitting in Mainwaring's office sipping champagne. Mainwaring lifted his glass to Mrs Runton. "It was your love of hoarding brown paper and string that won us the case," he said.

"Nonsense," said that practical woman. "But do tell me, Mr Mainwaring, what inspired you to see through that young man's scheme?"

"It wasn't inspiration," said Mainwaring. "Plain common-sense. If Paul was telling the truth, and I believed that he was, I had to find another explanation for the correspondence between Paul's book and Pank's life. There could be only one —that Pank had read the book and had purposely shaped his life to fit it. I confess that when I first saw STOGUMBER PANK over the shop, and the green canary, I had a horrid feeling that Paul must have seen it too, forgotten it with his conscious mind, but stored it up in his subconscious one. It's a thing that can and does happen. But when I got into the back room and saw Nelson and King Edward VII I knew my guess was right. Paul could hardly have forgotten a visit to the back room of a sweetshop, whereas Pank, with his thorough-ness, would have left no detail to chance. My worst moment was when Paul took so long to remember how any outsider could have had a leisurely look at his typescript."

"I was on my way home from Bagthorpe's," said Paul, "and forgot the thing on the bus from sheer elation. And since it was returned next day, I soon forgot all about it. In any case it was only the second copy. I left the top one with Bagthorpe."

"It's nice to think, isn't it," said Mainwaring, "that Bag-thorpe's five thousand pounds will enable Stogumber to pay our costs?"

They all agreed that it was very nice indeed.

A Slice of France

THE young soldier's photograph, framed in black, hung solitary upon the whitewashed wall. Above it drooped a small wreath of bay-leaves, freshly cut. On the bottom of the ebony frame was inscribed in letters of gold *"Mort pour la Patrie."* Below the frame again, on the mantelshelf too heavy for the small iron grate, a yellowing newspaper cutting, mounted and framed in black passe-partout, leant against the wall.

The photograph in itself was not impressive. It was an enlargement, slightly out of focus, from a snapshot. The young soldier, close-cropped, with thin long features, sulky mouth and frightened eyes, was capless, in fatigue dress. Behind him could be seen, with an imprecision that increased with distance, guy-ropes, trestles and the shapes of those enormous washtub-like vessels which encumber the entrance to a camp cookhouse.

Had it not been for the mischance that the only surviving portrait of a hero who died for his country was this snapshot of a scared young scullion peeling potatoes, the room, small and bare as it was, might have been taken for the shrine that Madame Pierre Marin, the soldier's mother, tried to make of it. It was she who regularly renewed the wreath of bay-leaves; she who, to discourage the use of the room for non-memorial purposes, as regularly removed from it the straight-backed straw-bottomed chairs with which her husband persisted in his attempts to furnish it.

For to Pierre Marin, the *patron*, this clean, unencumbered room, with its one great polished dresser of Spanish chestnut

57

wood, and its square oak table, was the very place in which to drink a liqueur with a friend or acquaintance. The cupboard below the dresser housed the bottle of Cointreau and the thick, diminutive tumblers in which he liked to serve it, and the photograph and newspaper-cutting afforded an easy, because visual, point of departure (as I was to learn) for his habitual monologue of complaint. And it was to this room that he led me, after a moment or two of, to me, embarrassing non-recognition, after I had knocked at the door of his rather dreadful little pre-fabricated home.

It was a year or two after Hitler's war, and I had found myself unexpectedly in the neighbourhood of St Michel, where the Esterel mountains peter out upon a red, rocky coast. In the early nineteen-thirties I had been obliged, for health reasons, to spend a winter and spring at St Michel with my young family, and of all the natives of that hospitable place none had become closer friends with, or more admired by, ourselves than the brothers Marin. Jean and Pierre Marin had kept the only bathing establishment— *"Etablissement de bains Frères Marin"*—a long row of wooden cabins, freshly painted, with a wooden jetty from the end of which the bolder bathers took headers, from the middle of which the less bold descended by a ladder, into the transparent, rock-bottomed sea.

Jean and Pierre were not natives of Provence. They were Bretons, tall, broad-shouldered, blue-eyed men, whose mahogany necks and shoulders contrasted vividly with their thin white singlets. They were jolly men, who greeted the children, scampering down the wooden gangway from the Parade, with a joyful cry of *"Ohé la jeunesse!"* Men whose deep voices and large masculine gestures made short work of any lingering myth at the back of a British mind that one Englishman is a match for five Frenchmen. Both had served in the French navy, as their upright, disciplined backs and torsos bore witness; and had it not been that Pierre's nose was a thought more aquiline, his hair a shade darker, than the nose and hair of his elder brother, it had not been easy to tell them apart. Our relations with this splendid pair soon became familiar; they even managed, as old navy men, to shepherd the whole family on board the *Villeneuve,* a light cruiser that anchored for two days not half a mile from the Lion de Mer; they advised us, to our profit, on what bait would tempt a squid from its cleft in the submerged, refracted rocks; they warned us, after one glance at the sky, of an approaching Mistral. During the bathing season we saw them every day.

Accordingly it was disappointing, and even, as I have said, embarrassing to find, on knocking at Pierre's door, that he did not recognise me until I had recalled to his mind half a dozen or more incidents from the past, vivid to myself but more than half forgotten by him. He did at last remember *"la jeunesse"* as a group but no individual names or characters, and although he invited me into his house, carried a couple of chairs into the "shrine" and produced the Cointreau and the glasses, I realised that it was an auditor for his own troubles, not an old friend, that he was making welcome.

That I was calling on Pierre and not on his elder brother Jean was a mere matter of chance. I had first visited the Parade, not exactly expecting, but half hoping, to find the *Etablissement Marin frères* still in existence. But there all was changed. An elaborate "Lido" had succeeded the wooden huts and jetty, and the young man at the *guichet,* in a smart white coat and peaked cap, only shook his head when I asked after the Marin brothers. Fortunately an elderly, salted old creature with a basket of wet towels came shuffling by in rope-soled slippers and, overhearing my question, good-naturedly paused to tell me that Pierre Marin lived in one of the new houses to the west of the port. Jean, too, was living in the town, but where he could not tell.

Pierre Marin, who looked far older than his age, scrawny, with a slight stoop, and with no light in his blue Breton eyes, made a gesture towards the photograph. "Our only son," he said (but *"unique"* has a more absolute, more forlorn overtone than "only"). Then, after filling the glasses, he picked up the framed cutting from the mantelshelf and put it into my hands. "The Marshal's very words," he said.

It was the report of a broadcast, in July 1940, by Marshal Pétain. It began, "Fathers and Mothers of France, it is to you I speak. In giving up the lives of your sons for the fatherland, you have given all you had. Your sublime sacrifice, your incomparable largesse, will be remembered so long as France endures. And she will endure. Although victory has been denied to us, your heroes did not die in vain." The broadcast continued in the old Marshal's habitual sombre, high-faluting, moralising vein so repulsive to his former allies, but, in the mouth of the hero of Verdun, far from unacceptable to a stunned and defeated people. To Pierre Marin and his wife such rhetoric had brought, it was clear, both pride and consolation.

I handed the cutting back to Pierre with such sympathetic grunts as I could contrive, and he began his monologue. As a former navy man, too old for active service, he had been conscripted as a labourer in the dockyard at Toulon. He had been over-worked, half-starved. He did not spare me his views on Oran and the desertion of the British air force which had contributed to the heroic death in action of the *unique* son. I had not the heart to argue with him: besides, it would have been useless. With French omniscience, he knew. He was now working at a petrol station on the Fréjus road, with little enough money. His wife washed linen twice a week at the Grand Hotel. And to think that, had it not been for Jean's betrayal of them, he would today be working their own land in Brittany!—rich land, a hundred and fifty hectares not far from Pontivy. Did I know Pontivy?

I did not, but his question interrupted his own flow of embittered grumblings and gave me a chance of pin-pointing his astonishing reference to Jean.

"Jean's betrayal of you?" I said. "I don't understand."

"How could you," he said, "since we ourselves have never

understood it. Just imagine, Monsieur, my own brother, my partner in business, my best friend! To do such a thing to us, at our time of mourning, at the moment of our great sacrifice! To destroy all our hopes, and to condemn us to this dog's life!" He expressed a dog's life in one great sweeping gesture.

The story was a long one. It began with a complicated history of former Marins, of marriages and dowries and deaths of great uncles, and ended with the decease, in the summer of 1940, of Aunt Amélie. It had been expected that Aunt Amélie, the last owner of the good land near Pontivy, would leave it to her nephews, Jean and Pierre, jointly, but in fact she had left it to Jean. Not that this had much mattered. The two brothers had often discussed that possibility, and Jean, who was not a marrying man, had made no secret of his intention to work the farm with Pierre as his partner, and to leave it to his nephew, that same young man who had died for his country. And then— who could believe it?—when the property was his own, Jean had promptly sold it for cash, and no less promptly given the proceeds away.

"Pouf! Like that! The family land, the old family house, everything gone, vanished! What do you think of that, Monsieur? Was there ever such a betrayal?"

I did not know what to think. I remembered Jean's honest blue eyes, his straightforward ways, the obvious affection between the two jovial brothers who had so endeared themselves to us all in the days gone by.

"What does Jean say about it?" I asked. "He must have had his reasons?"

Pierre shrugged his shoulders.

"How should I know?" he said. "I have never spoken to him since. I had this letter from him—I was in the dockyard at Toulon and I did not even answer it."

"But he must have given some explanation in his letter."

"There was some nonsense, I believe, about the war and sacrifice, as if we had not made sacrifice enough in giving our boy." He gestured towards the photograph. "Besides, what good can you do to your country by giving a slice of it away? A good Frenchman nourishes his corner of our land. He doesn't liquidate it."

"A man can do what he likes with his own, I suppose," I said, lamely enough.

"That, Monsieur, was what the lawyer said. But Jean and I were partners, we had everything in common. And the old Marshal was right"—he waved towards the newspaper cutting —"France bases herself on the family. To betray the family is to betray France."

I began to feel irritated with Pierre. The high-flown stuff, coupled with old Pétain, turned me towards Jean's side of the affair.

"They tell me Jean is living here in St Michel?"

"Yes. But we look the other way if we happen to meet."

"Can you give me his address?"

"Number 2, Rue Mistral, I believe."

"What does he do?"

"How should I know? He isn't starving."

I got up from my chair.

"Thank you," I said, "for your hospitality, Monsieur Pierre. I am truly sorry for all your misfortunes. It was a cruel war."

"You speak the truth," he said, shaking hands. "You others, safe in your island——"

I cut him short.

"We did come over here, you know."

"Under the command of an American," said Pierre.

"Luckily for you," I said. "*Adieu,* Monsieur." I could not say "*Au revoir.*"

The Mistral had risen as I turned away to look for the street that shared its name with that hateful wind. The dust was in my eyes, and the shutters rattled dismally on the houses overhead. I had listened to a sad story, and was dissatisfied with myself for my lack of wholehearted sympathy with the victim. It is annoying when one to whom pity is due puts one's back up.

St Michel is not a large town, and I had no difficulty in finding the Rue Mistral, a dusty, unkempt street in which tall
apartment-houses alternated with squat workshops and
stretches of white wall, over which an occasional rough-coated
palm could be seen wrestling with the gale. There was no
concierge at No. 2, but a cropped infant in a blouse told me
that Monsieur Marin lived on the fifth to which he had just
mounted. I climbed the stairs and knocked at a door on which
was nailed a neat shiny card inscribed "Marin."

Jean opened to me, with an expression as blankly enquiring
as Pierre's had been. Jean, too, had fallen away in face and
neck and overall bulk; he was a thin brown man, but he did not
stoop like his younger brother, and he looked as hard as sea-
soned timber. As with Pierre, I had to recall this and that in
the past before the light of recognition came into his eyes; when
it did so, the grasp of his hand was strong and friendly.

"Come in, Monsieur," he said, "and sit down. I was just about
to eat, and coffee is ready."

The room itself was spick and span, with several pieces of
good old Provençal furniture, but Jean's midday meal, consisting of half a double *flute* of greyish bread, cheese and a
plate of cold runner-beans soaked in oil, explained his fine-
drawn frame. As Pierre had said, Jean was not starving, but it
was clear that he was living near the bone.

I sat down and while Jean was busy for a few moments with
the coffee simmering on a primus-stove, I had a chance of
studying him. He had been, as I have said, the most jovial of
men, full of life and humour, as indeed had Pierre. But whereas the younger brother's once genial features had been trans-
muted into a mask of discontent and self-pity, with the corners
of his mouth fixedly down-drawn, Jean's new face was one of
profound unhappiness, of a frozen dismay. There was a look
of astonishment in his blue eyes, as of a man who, once
appalled, had remained appalled.

He came back from the stove with two cups of coffee—and
very good coffee it was—and sat himself at the table.

"Monsieur will forgive me if I eat," he said. "Work does not wait."

I asked him about his work. In the season, he said, he was odd-man at the Grand Hotel, he also took visitors out in the boat for sea-fishing. "But the fish in this blue sea are nothing," he added. "They serve for amusement, but for real fish you must have the green seas, the seas of our Brittany. With those a man can nourish himself."

"Did you never think of going back to Brittany, Monsieur Jean?" I asked him.

For a moment there was a gleam in his eye.

"Ah, Monsieur," he said. "Had it not been for the war! We should have gone back. But not to fish. We Marins were never fishermen, Monsieur. We belonged to the land, and the land has belonged to us. Rich land, corn and pasture, everything but vines. You had only to bend your back to grow rich as Onassis."

The gleam died out, and the look of dismay returned. I was determined to get to the bottom of the "betrayal" story.

"I saw Pierre this morning," I said.

"My poor brother," he said. "Did he talk to you?"

"Yes, he did."

Jean dropped his eyes, fumbling with his bread like a child scolded at table.

"Then you know everything," he said.

"I know Pierre's story," I said. "But not everything. There are usually two sides to a case, aren't there?"

"I was crazy," he said. "But you know how it is. In a time of catastrophe, a man loses his head. I should have thought of Pierre, of course. But when the blow fell——" he completed his sentence with a gesture of hopelessness.

I nodded sympathetically.

"An only boy," I said.

Jean looked up at me quickly. His eyes were quizzical, almost amused.

"Oh that!" he said. "You have seen the 'shrine'? Let me

64

tell you, then. That poor boy was no good. Spoilt from the first. Did you meet my sister-in-law?"

"No," I said.

"Pierre could do nothing against her. He was too soft. She let the boy rot—he never did a hand's turn in his life. Did you hear how they 'gave' him to the fatherland?"

I nodded.

"Gave him my foot! There wasn't a string to be pulled that she didn't pull to keep the boy out of the Army. There was this cousin in the Postes et Télégraphes—he knew the Deputy for Draguignan, who had a *tuyau* to the Minister. It was quite a history, I can tell you. And when that wouldn't work, she tried the doctors. I don't say the boy was a-hundred-per-cent fit. Young men in a blue funk seldom are. She paid I don't know what to a psychiatrist. He used some long words from what I hear. But that wouldn't work either. In the end the Army took him and put him in the cook-house. The hero never got within a hundred miles of any fighting. The Boches bombed his camp and that was that. Poor boy, he was never a Marin. One doesn't like to say it, Monsieur, of one's own flesh and blood, but the 'gift' of that young man was a gift of so much rubbish."

For the first time I felt rather thankful to old Pétain. At least he had succeeded in bandaging the parents' eyes. Jean had stopped to munch; the look of amused contempt faded from his eyes and the old dismay reappeared in them.

"No, Monsieur," he said. "It was after the Armistice had been signed that I lost my head. I was working in the ship-yards at Villefranche. There were no Boches there as yet, and we could listen to the wireless. I heard de Gaulle speaking from London. And believe me, that man put all thoughts of duty out of my head. Every Frenchman must do what he can, he said. So I asked myself what could I do? I was too old to fight; as a naval reservist I was working, although as a mere labourer, under discipline. But if there was little I could do, there was something I could give. Pierre told you of course of Aunt Amélie's bequest?"

"Yes," I said.

"I went to a lawyer, a relation of mine and an honest man. I told him to sell the property near Pontivy for what it would fetch, and to give the proceeds to the chiefs of the local resistance. It was a tidy sum, as you can imagine. A hundred and fifty hectares of the best land, undevastated! Not that I had hoped for half as much as I got—there was the war, after all, and the fixed prices. But it seems that not even a Boche can fix prices for a Breton. Anyway, the buyers came up like carp to a crumb, and the General's resistance got a small fortune in cash. And they really did get it. My lawyer knew all the ropes. After the war they sent me a receipt and the formal thanks of de Gaulle himself. Engraved." He paused to sip his coffee.

"A proud possession," I said.

"A certificate of lunacy," said Jean, sharply. He put down the cup and looked me full in the face. "Monsieur," he said, "when that bit of paper reached me I tore it into twenty pieces. I was ashamed, you see."

"Ashamed of having helped your country to victory with all you had?"

"Oh as for that, Monsieur, when the Boche came to occupy us here I did my bit in the local resistance. There wasn't much to be done down here, naturally—some little bits of sabotage —not too badly executed, although I say it as shouldn't. But a man's life is his own. If I liked to risk it—and there were some little moments, of course—those devils of gendarmes were worse than the Boche, believe me—that was my own affair. But the land was a trust. A trust, Monsieur, that I betrayed. Carried away, like a crazy fool, by a few words spoken by de Gaulle in London! He's a spell-binder, of course, but at my age, to let myself forget my duty! No, Monsieur, I shall never get over it."

"And when did you first repent of your patriotism?" I asked, cold as ice.

He was deeply offended.

"Do you ask that of an old member of the resistance?" he said. "Are you demanding a catalogue of the risks I ran—I, who once served in the Navy? Old sailors neither boast nor repent of their patriotism, believe me."

I began to understand, yet without understanding, the mind of this strange, unhappy man.

"I beg your pardon," I said. "I should have asked you, when did you first repent of your munificence?"

"When Pierre failed to answer my letter," he said. "They took time, you see, these transactions, and only when I finally heard that the farm was sold and the money in the hands of the Gaullists did I write to explain the whole matter to Pierre. That the letter had reached him I know—for the man who carried it to Toulon returned to tell me so. 'There is no answer,' he said. It was then that my eyes were opened. I can tell you I was appalled."

"My old friend," I said. "I wish you could explain it to me. At the moment of catastrophe, on a fine, generous impulse, you did a fine, generous thing. What can be so appalling in that?"

"Because, Monsieur, I lost my head and failed to distinguish. Give your all to France, said the General, and I saw France, under the spell of his eloquence, as a beautiful woman— a woman in distress, a woman who, besides, was the mother of us all. But had I stopped to reason, Monsieur, had I distinguished, I should have seen that the real France is no woman, but the land, the land beneath our feet. How can you give to France land that is already France, that is part of herself? It makes no sense. My family had the luck to own a few hectares of France. When it came to my turn to possess it, I had but one duty: to make the most of it, not to let it fall into the hands of who knows what speculators, what profiteers, or at best what ignoramuses? No, Monsieur, I betrayed both our land and my family. That is the thought I have to live with."

"I think Pierre should forgive you all the same," I said.

"What good would that be to me, when I cannot forgive myself?" He got up from the table, wiping his mouth with a spotted handkerchief. "You must pardon me, Monsieur, but I shall be late for work."

I also rose.

"I see that there is nothing I can say," I mumbled. "Except how much I feel for you. It was a cruel war."

"You speak the truth," he said. "You others, secure in your island, guarded by the good sea ..."

I cut him short.

"We did come over here, you know," I said.

"Under the command of a General Eisenhower," he said.

"Luckily for you," I said. "*Adieu,* Monsieur Jean."

I could not say "*Au revoir.*"

Thoughts at a Memorial Service

HAD there been a larger and heavier type available, the evening papers would doubtless have preferred it to the one used by them as headlines on the day, in late August, when Mr Charles Mostyn, the Chancellor of the Exchequer, shot the Prime Minister dead. The shooting, which needless to say was a pure accident, had taken place on one of Lord Kilspindie's grouse-moors in Perthshire. Lord Kilspindie, a gentle-minded Conservative who believed in the efficient grace of "getting together," had invited Henry Crabbe, the Prime Minister, and his Chancellor of the Exchequer to the same shooting party, because of his conviction that on a Scotch moor, in the presence of the everlasting hills, and in the shared enjoyment of their favourite sport, the notorious strain between these two men would relax into ease, if not amity. Unfortunately his theory was never put to the test. For on the very first morning, during the second drive, one of them slew the other.

Nobody present except the victim himself could have explained how it happened that an experienced shot like the Prime Minister could have left his butt, even though the drive was almost over, to gather a dead bird behind the line. It is true that the bird lay in a hollow behind a heathery knoll which may have appeared to the dead man to offer complete protection from the adjoining butt. It was also remembered that the line of beaters had lost formation over some rough and hag-ridden ground, with the result that those on the extreme right, opposite the Prime Minister in his butt on the extreme left, came up to the butts well ahead of the main body. But, whatever his miscalculations, nothing could excuse a gun for leaving his butt until the drive, from end to end of the line, was indubitably over. That the hollow behind the heathery knoll was not fifteen yards from Mostyn's butt made his action still more extraordinary. But to that hollow the Prime Minister went, unseen by his neighbour, and when a last grouse came swooping to Mostyn's left, too low to be shot in front, Mostyn had every right to fire at it as it crossed, rising slightly, the top of the knoll. As he fired, the Prime Minister's head and neck, in profile, rose directly between barrel and bird, and some pellets, striking him full in the side of the neck, penetrated the carotid artery.

Charles Mostyn was not a weak or a sentimental character. He must have known, even in the first instant of shocked dismay, that he had not been to blame. But there are sights so horrifying, circumstances so cruel, that to have been physically responsible for them, however blamelessly, sickens and shakes a sensitive man to a point where the question of guilt or innocence becomes irrelevant. So it was with Mostyn. Back in Kilspindie's lodge, unable to eat or sleep, he had, in the course of twenty-four hours, built up an image of himself as a man apart, cursed, with blood upon his head. In vain did his wife, Lady Hermione, and his kind host reiterate that not a living soul was holding him responsible for what had been the sheerest accident. In vain did compassionate telegrams from friends and colleagues condole with, and acquit, him. The wretched man was obsessed: firstly, by a picture that hung, as it were, in the air before him night and day, of the welling arterial blood upon the heather, and, secondly, by the thought that the man he had killed had never been his friend, and that by his death he, Mostyn, must almost inevitably step into his victim's shoes. That, he decided, he never could, or would do.

His wife and host, shocked and saddened as they were, had

no such reason, as he, to lose their sense of proportion. But they guessed and were alarmed at his state of mind, and when, a couple of days later, the verdict of the coroner's jury was "Accidental Death," with a rider that not a scintilla of blame attached to any person but the victim himself, they did their utmost to persuade the unhappy Mostyn that, publicly exculpated, he was as fit and as free to serve in any capacity as before.

But Mostyn, his first shock of horror aggravated by bouts of insomnia alternating with nightmares, was not to be persuaded. As soon as the funeral of his late leader, which took place privately in the country, was accomplished, he sat down and wrote to the King's private secretary. Sir Arthur Little was an old friend, from whom he had received a note of condolence and concern. To him Mostyn now opened his heart, explaining that, sheer accident as the affair had been, it was impermissible that a position should arise where it could be said of a public man that he had obtained promotion by shooting his chief. He made no pretence of not recognising his claim to the first place in the Government. By ability, by seniority, by experience, he had no rival in the Cabinet. But he must ask Arthur to tell the Monarch that, while willing to retain his present post, he could not allow his name to be considered for the Premiership.

Parliament was in recess and would not meet again until October; the political scene was tranquil, and there was no hurry to appoint Henry Crabbe's successor. In any case the King felt that nothing should be done until after the memorial service for the late Prime Minister had been held in Westminster Abbey.

About a fortnight after the shooting, in the middle of September, the memorial service took place. It was attended naturally by the whole Cabinet. But Mostyn found it altogether beyond him to take his proper place on the right of the first rows reserved for Ministers. The certainty that every eye would be upon him, to mark how the man who had fired the fatal shot would deport himself, was not to be borne. Attend he must, but he decided to take a modest place, far from the central aisle, and many rows to the rear, a place where his face would be seen only by those whose curiosity should overcome their sense of reverence and good manners. In such an assembly on such an occasion, these were likely to be few indeed.

Mostyn and his wife reached the Abbey early, and took up their obscure position. He himself had been careful, at the entrance, to make sure that the reporters should note his name, since he would not be seen at the side of his colleagues.

The Mostyns seated themselves, he not watching the slow whispering crowds that gradually darkened the floor of the great abbey, but attempting to listen to the voluntary. But the chosen music was a Prelude by Bach, discovering so delicate and joyous an air against a manly reassuring bass, that Mostyn could not suppress a thought of how unsuitable, how almost comically inept, such music was to the personality of the dead man. In fact, it provoked him, upsetting, from the very start, the proper mood for the coming service, and setting off in him an involuntary train of meditation ill-suited to the time and the occasion.

"This ravishing air for old Crabbe!" he thought. "Soldiers' Chorus would have been more the thing: 'brown boots and mulligatawny soup!' Crabbe was always a trampler—trampled me time and again; bulldozing. Bulldozed me out of being President of the Union. I made rings round him in the debates. Flashy speaker—no facts, no arrangement. I suppose I must have been too sure of myself. But *I* had to work; he didn't. In and out of all the colleges, speaking at all their potty little societies, getting to know everybody, dear old Crabby, while I was swotting at Bradley's *Logic*. I doubt if he could have understood a word of it. And beats me by sixty-four votes! Sheer bulldozing."

Lady Hermione lightly touched his sleeve. The Beadle and the Dean were coming up the aisle, escorting the King's representative, a minor Royalty. Behind them came Sir Arthur Little. But Mostyn was away with his thoughts.

"Once a wire-puller, always a wire-puller. How he got that safe seat at Mudlington, God knows. While I had to fight East Snape and the Claypoles without a dog's chance. The door marked Push and the door marked Pull. Good old Crabby, always in by one or the other. Had that uncle, of course. And to be fair to him, given a chance, he could take it. Almost spellbound *me* once or twice. Something likeable about Crabbe—till you got to know him. And clever as a monkey. Could play a bad hand which I never could. Never afraid of bluffing. Nor of playing a dirty trick either. That Carlton Club meeting. Gad, I was a simpleton! I can remember his note now, every word of it. 'My dear Charles, I don't think you and I need pretend not to know that the choice of a successor to dear old B.K. will fall upon one or the other of us. We can hardly vote for ourselves next Tuesday, so how would it be if we proposed one another? It would look well; show that, whoever wins, the other will support him, and add a touch of grace to our proceedings. Yours ever, Harry.' "

His wife tugged at his sleeve this time. He was the last to stand up for the hymn, number 470. She put the service paper into his hand. But Mostyn was at the party meeting at the Carlton Club, three years ago.

"What an innocent I was! Didn't even consult my friends. Never occurred to me that I shouldn't succeed B.K. Had the dear old boy not been unconscious from that stroke he would, Elsie has always assured me, have advised the King to send for me. Always spoke of me, she said, as his destined successor. Even so, might not have been a party meeting at all, but for Crabbe's busy persistence. 'Party must choose our leader; not fair on the Crown; precedents; Bonar Law case.' Buttonholed everybody. Largely my own fault, of course. Had I been less sure of myself, less aloof, less shy—my absurd false modesty—I might have heard something, been put on my guard. As it was I fell into the trap and agreed to Crabbe's proposal—'to add a touch of grace!'—Good lord! How like Harry, how like me!

"God, that meeting! Quite a fair crowd in the room. Crabbe

arrives with Kilspindie who takes the Chair. Crabbe plumps down next to him. Moving little speech about B.K. from Kilspindie, bless his simple heart! Kilspindie sits down and whispers to Crabbe. Crabbe shakes his head—not for him to put himself forward, oh no! He says something to Kilspindie who calls on me. Up I get, like a fool, and formally propose Mr Henry Crabbe as leader of the party. I sit down. Uneasy pause. 'Any seconder?' asks the Chairman. Another pause, then a back-bencher seconds and sits down. Kilspindie sits looking like a lost dog. Crabbe whispers to him again. Up gets the guileless K and says 'Those in favour hold up their hands.' Up go hands from about a quarter of the room. All eyes are upon me. I, the mover, hadn't raised my own hand! In my confusion, lose my head and raise my hand in a brisk, decisive way—taken, I heard afterwards, as a studied, emphatic gesture purposely delayed so as to be seen by everybody! Coupled with the taking of a vote with only one name before the meeting, the whole performance was thought to have been pre-arranged! And so it was, by God! Never saw so many puzzled faces, or so much whispering. But if Mostyn, for some private reason, won't stand, all right. Let's make a show of unity. In the end, slowly and reluctantly, a majority of the hands go up. 'Those against?' says Kilspindie, after another word from his prompter. Nobody stirs. Kilspindie declares Crabbe elected: some feeble applause, a louder buzz of talk, and everybody drifts out. I too stupefied to speak to a soul. Next day, Monarch sends for Crabbe."

A wave of sheer misery, such as had so often visited him in sleepless nights, again possessed him at the memory of this farcical and fatal assembly. His reverie was momentarily broken by it. He could actually hear the trebles singing a verse of the hymn on their own:

"Father-like he tends and spares us."

"He didn't tend or spare *me*," thought Mostyn, "nor to be fair, did he tend or spare Crabbe that day on the moors— oh God! oh God!" The picture of the dying man, which

74

had faded of late even from his dreams all but returned to unman him once more, forcing him to clutch, if only to ward off a visible tremor, at the thought of Crabbe's trickiness and falsity. "And now," he thought, "he's done me down again. Why the devil couldn't he have stayed in his butt?"

The hymn was over. His wife pulled him down to his knees. But by now Mostyn was past praying or praying for. He was thinking of his letter to Arthur Little, and the folly of it. Then he suddenly prayed after all: "Pray God it's not too late!" Nobody had been sent for so far: "I've only to retract what I wrote when beside myself with shock, and all may be well yet."

Now everybody was standing up once more: the choir were singing the hundred and twenty-first psalm. Mostyn, with hope renewed, was momentarily able to follow the words

> "So that the sun shall not burn thee by day
> Neither the moon by night."

He all but giggled. "How exactly like one of old Crabbe's perorations!" he thought. "Magnificent sound: entirely meaningless. How could the moon burn anybody by night? But the Psalmist has always got away with it. So did Crabbe, even at his woolliest. Wasn't his mother Welsh?"

Mostyn was feeling better: to have smiled at his dead rival was a big step towards recovery. His eyes sought the back of Sir Arthur Little's head.

"Must catch him after the service," he thought. "I can slip out easily enough by the side aisle. People won't move till H.R.H. has left."

His gaze shifted to where his colleagues stood in the front row. On the right of the line, next to the empty chair which had been reserved for himself, rose the heavy, rounded shoulders, the fleshy neck, the round sleek head of Algernon Blunt, the Home Secretary.

"Smug," thought Mostyn, "that's what he is, smug. Never knew the back of a head could be smug!" Till today Mostyn had accepted, with utter apathy, the probability that Blunt would be Crabbe's successor. Now, suddenly, it appeared absurd. "Man's a mediocrity: good chap, but nothing to him. Algy for P.M.? Never!"

Down on his knees he bent for a prayer and responses, his bowed head full of Algy's shortcomings. Then, seated again for the Lesson, he found himself actually listening to *"Let us now praise famous men."*

"Famous? Henry Crabbe? Notorious perhaps. 'Let us now praise notorious men'—no, it doesn't go. Yet L-G was both famous and notorious. Could *I* ever be famous? I've not had my chance yet. To be famous you must have nerves, strength, self-control. Not throw in your hand because you've had a shock. But what famous men have shot a colleague by mistake? Oh God—oh God—it wasn't fair. But that's all done with. Harry's fault entirely, poor fool. Not mine. Everybody knows that."

The congregation stood up again, for a hymn. Once more Mostyn could scan the row of his colleagues.

"I shall keep Algy at the Home Office all the same. But I must get rid of Bogie from F.O. Puts the Yanks' hackles up. A Viscounty for him, I think, and the Privy Seal. He'll kick, of course. What luck that Cantuar is retiring next month! I know what I shall do there—nasty shock for Ebor—but look at him, just look at him, poor old sheep."

Mostyn was beginning to enjoy himself. He began to join in the singing:

"They fly forgotten, as a dream
Dies at the opening day."

"Forgotten," he thought, "what a mercy forgetfulness is. How long before Crabbe's forgotten? Six months? A year! Perceval was shot, but nobody's ever thought about him since. Crabbe's not a Perceval, of course. He could make a speech. But who remembers speeches?"

The last hymn ended and the congregation knelt for a closing prayer and collect. Mostyn had been to many memorial ser-

76

vices, and in most cases the widow or family had had a say in the choice of prayers. But Crabbe having been a bachelor, leaving few to mourn him, his executors had left the order of service to the clergy, who liked to stick to the prayer-book. So it was with no little surprise that Mostyn, whom a touch of shame for his wandering thoughts had recalled to the matter on hand, heard the officiating priest intoning, loudly and clearly:

> We give Thee hearty thanks for that it has pleased Thee to deliver this our brother out of the miseries of this sinful world.

Mostyn could hardly refrain from an audible and immediate Amen, so hearty were his own thanks, hitherto frankly suppressed but, during the last half hour, struggling for expression. He bowed his head for the final Blessing in a glow of contentment. He had Mother Church's sanction for a sense of gratitude, which, without it, he had never dared acknowledge even to his secret self.

The service was over, but the congregation remained, for a time, in their seats. The slow, deliberate emergence of the clergy and choristers from their stalls; the building up of the procession, with the two Archbishops at its tail, for the solemn exit; the return of the beadles and Dean to escort His Royal Highness from the Abbey—all this weaving and counter-weaving of expressionless white-clad figures took time. Meanwhile the organist had struck up with Chopin's Funeral March. And when Mostyn heard that poignant, familiar, over-sweet threnody, there came back to him, uninvited, the words to which he and his friends had chanted it in his ribald youth: *"Ne soyez pas si bête, Em-ma! Ne soyez pas si bête, Em-ma!"* They came to him as an omen, a last, small, clinching, admonition not to be a sentimental fool but to go boldly to meet his destiny.

Yes, this was the moment to go. Arthur Little had turned about, obviously intending to follow close upon the heels of

H.R.H. Mostyn whispered "Come" to his wife, and glided away down the aisle. No need for any unbecoming haste, since H.R.H.'s snail-like procession was setting the pace for Little. Mostyn was among the first to reach the porch; there could be no question of the Private Secretary escaping him.

Sir Arthur Little had no wish to escape Mostyn. On the contrary, he no sooner saw him than he turned towards him, hand outstretched.

"My dear Charles, I hoped I should see you. You'll find a letter from me at your house, but I wanted just to tell you how damned sorry I am. The Monarch has written to you, too: he couldn't be more upset about it. But as he said: 'Charles is right, as usual. It's hellish bad luck, but I just can't have it said that my Prime Minister shot his way into the job.' You're an angel to say you'll stay on. The King's sending for Algy Blunt to-morrow morning."

Little gave Mostyn's hand an affectionate squeeze and melted into the throng now pouring from the Abbey.

It was all over. As sudden a death as Crabbe's. Mostyn caught a fleeting glimpse of Blunt, the mediocre Blunt, getting into a car. "He's seven years younger than I am," he thought, "and fit as a fiddle. He doesn't even shoot."

Founder's Kin

QUARLES COLLEGE, Oxford, as few, if any, schoolboys know, enjoyed, or suffered from, a peculiar, indeed a unique constitution. As in the case of the Masters of Magdalene College, Cambridge, its Wardens were appointed, not by the Fellows, but by the reigning head of the Founder's family. In the case of Quarles, however, the grip of the dead hand of the Founder was firmer and more constricting than in the case of Magdalene. For not only did the head of the Quarles family appoint the Warden, but he was constrained, by the Founder's Statute, to appoint a blood-relation of the original Quarles, should there be any such alive, of age, in their right mind and "*litteratus*". (By a decision of the King's Bench, confirmed on appeal, in 1743, it was ruled that "*litteratus*" meant "able to read and write.")

The founder had been Thomas Quarles, a favourite and creature of Thomas Cromwell, who rewarded him for his prowess in robbing the Church with valuable grants of the purloined lands. He further contrived to obtain a barony from King Henry VIII for his part in bringing his former patron to the block. Looking back, in his declining years, to his early career, it occurred to him (for he was no fool) that his conduct in both these affairs had not been what we should nowadays call pretty. Quarles, finding the ethics of the Enlightenment beyond him, had always adhered inconspicuously to the Old Religion, and he now consulted his Confessor. This good man agreed with him, at any rate respecting the Cromwellian period of his past.

79

He confirmed all of Quarles's forebodings about Hell; but pointed out a way of escape. Let Lord Rudham (for that was his title) build and endow a College for godly learning, and thereby save his soul from the pit. The penitent old peer, feeling that the premium for Eternal Life Insurance could hardly be too high, made a truly handsome restitution. The two outwardly charming, and inwardly uncomfortable, Tudor quadrangles of Quarles College were completed in 1576, and his nephew, Henry Quarles, installed as Warden in the dark, but richly panelled, Lodge. For Lord Rudham, in making his lordly contribution to godly learning, saw no reason why his own descendants should not take a moderate rake-off from his bounty. Hence the Statute about Founder's Kin. Henry Quarles, for all that he had been a soldier of fortune, could undoubtedly read and write, and although he soon found the Lodge too dark, and the climate of Oxford disagreeable, his emoluments enabled him to avoid both by the payment of a scholarly Sub-Warden to look after the College.

It is much to the credit of the Quarles family that, in the first decade of the twentieth century, a descendant of Thomas Quarles, appointed by a Lord Rudham, should have been presiding, with dignity and success, over the college that bore his name. But at the time of the incident I am about to describe, Warden Bascombe (whose mother had been a Quarles) had lately died, and the Fellows were awaiting, without either excitement or apprehension, the appointment of his successor. That Lord Rudham would choose Dr Angus McGregor (whose grandmother had been a Quarles) seemed certain, but Lord Rudham was at the moment shooting big game in East Africa, and it was probable that his mind was running more on Game-wardens than on the Collegiate kind.

My story opens on a night in the first week of June. Some of the Fellows of the College were sitting, supping port wine, in that graceful William and Mary Common Room which looks out upon the New Quadrangle (built in 1701). The month being June, they were sitting at a horseshoe table before a glowing coal fire, drinking their port from a decanter which passed from the Fellow on the left to the Fellow on the right of the fireplace by means of a fascinating little ebony carriage which, drawn by a cord, ran on silver rails the length of the chimney-piece.

In the middle of the horseshoe sat the Dean, Mr Dunton, known as "Dusty" from the colour of his hair; a man of precise and measured speech who, but for the twinkle in his grey eyes, might have been thought formidable. On one side of him sat Professor Ryburgh, the charm of whose Scots tongue made up for the untidiness of his drooping grey moustache; on the other, bolt upright, was Mr Barsham, the Grecian, with whom you had to be careful, for he could bite. At either end of the table, to manage the railway, sat the cherubic Heseltine and the cadaverous Pratt, the Junior Fellow.

But they were not enjoying that "good talk" for which Oxford Common Rooms were, in those days, celebrated. On the contrary, they were discussing, with concerned, anxious expressions and some heat, the reason for a College Meeting which Dunton had called for ten o'clock on the following morning. What had happened was this. Two days previously an undergraduate, Henry Quarles, a nephew of Lord Rudham, had celebrated his coming-of-age with a "twenty-firster." The dinner had taken place out of College, but the party had afterwards adjourned, in somewhat more than high spirits, to Henry's rooms. Henry himself, being in training as stroke of the College Eight, was perfectly sober, but some of his friends were not, and all were in the mood for a "rag." From Henry's rooms it was possible to see, across the Little Quad, into the well-lighted ground-floor rooms of the new Bursar, T. B. Trout. One of the windows was open, and the sleek black head of the Bursar could be seen, back to the window, bent over the papers on which he was working.

"Who's little bloody?" asked one of the out-of-college diners.

"It's the Bursar, Trout," said Henry.

"Good chap?"

"No," said Henry. "Typical heygate."

(It must be explained that fifty years ago the word "heygate" was in current use at Oxford to describe the prim, the priggish and the conventional. T. B. Trout was all of these.)

"Then let's fish for Trout."

This proposal, suggested as much, perhaps, by the fishing-rods and landing-net in a corner of Henry's room as by the Bursar's name, was applauded by the whole party as the very thing. It was decided that Henry, as the only skilful fisherman present, should cast a lure, about the size of a man's hand and made of tin-foil and paper, through the Bursar's window and over his head, while Philpotts, the most sober of the party after Henry, should stand by the window with the landing-net ready to pounce should the fish follow the lure as it was withdrawn. It took some little time to make a satisfactory lure, and still more for Henry to practise casting, with this unaccustomed object at the end, in a dark corner of the quadrangle. But Henry was a good dry-fly fisherman, equal to dropping a fly beneath the overhanging branches of a willow tree, and, having got the feel of the thing, he crept towards the Bursary on rubber soles, while Philpotts, hugging the wall, sidled up to the open window with the landing-net held like a butterfly net at the ready. The rest of the party, having put out the lights, crowded the two windows of Henry's room.

Henry had not spent so many days of his young life on the Itchen for nothing. He made a perfect low, sideways cast. The lure flew through the window, skimmed over the Bursar's head, and landed in his inkpot. For a second, the Bursar stared at it, uncomprehending. But when it began to crawl towards him and over his papers, trailing ink, and he felt the gentle rubbing of a fishing-line between his left ear and his head, he guessed, and he clutched. Henry struck, gently, and began reeling in, giving the Trout plenty of time to rise, to turn, to move towards the window. By now the hour was late, and the quadrangle was almost in darkness but for the part illuminated by the lights of the Bursary itself. When the Bursar reached the window, still clutching the lure, he could see only the fishing line and the tip of a rod. In order to discover the holder of the rod he had to lean out over the sill. He leant out. Down came the landing-net, enmeshing his head and jolting his teeth as his pipe was jerked out of his mouth.

"Got him!" shouted Philpotts. "And by Jove it's a whopper."

The party in Henry's room cheered. Henry and Philpotts clung together in helpless laughter. But the Bursar, not unnaturally, was as far from being amused as a man can well be.

The reason for the College Meeting, then, to be held at ten o'clock on the morrow of the conversation round the Common Room fire, was to send Henry down. And the reason for the conversation being heated was that it was Eights Week, that Henry, who had his Blue, was stroking the College Eight, and that the Eight had more than a good chance of going Head of the River for the first time in the history of Quarles College. Many of the Fellows, including Dusty Dunton himself, felt that Henry's punishment might, in those circumstances, be postponed until after the last night of the bumping races. He had played a silly, childish trick, but it was not criminal; he had made a full and humble apology to Trout, and that the best college boat Quarles had ever put on the river, and the College itself, should forgo so great a glory rather than give a few days' grace to the graceless, seemed rather absurd. But there was one immovable obstacle to this sensible course: the Bursar.

To enter fully into the Bursar's feelings you must be called Trout; you must have had, and still have, spots on your face which had been, throughout your schooldays, associated with your surname; you must be entirely devoid of any sense of humour; you must have the highest opinion of your own abilities, and of the dignity and importance of the office of College Bursar; you must despise all forms of athletics, and you must have a dislike for all hearty young men. Only with these characteristics will you be able to understand and sympathise with T. B. Trout's attitude to this unfortunate affair.

Dusty Dunton had appealed to him. Professor Ryburgh had walked him seven times round the Big Quadrangle after dinner; even the unathletic Barsham had been to his rooms to attempt to bring him to reason. But Trout was adamant. Henry Quarles must be sent down, and at once, or he, Trout, would himself resign his Fellowship and the Bursary.

The slight heat referred to in the conversation at the horse-shoe table had occurred when Heseltine and Pratt had joined together in saying "Then let Trout go!" This had called forth a rebuke from the Dean, on which the Professor and Barsham had supported him.

"I stand by my Fellows," Dunton had said. "Trout has served, and is serving, the College admirably—we have never had a better Bursar. He did nothing whatever to provoke this inexcusable assault upon him. And I shall expect all the Fellows—*all*, do you hear, Heseltine?—do you hear, Pratt?—to stand by our colleague at tomorrow's meeting."

That was that, and the five men were at one again in bemoaning the hard fate of the College Eight, who, with a substitute stroke, could at best hope to keep their place on the river, when the College butler entered the room and noiselessly approached the Dean.

"Yes, Stibbard?"

"Mr Henry Quarles, sir. Very anxious to speak to you at once, sir."

"He must know I can't see him here."

"Between ourselves, and quite *sub rosa*, the young gentleman seems to have something on his mind, sir."

"I've no doubt he has. But this is not the place to get it off his mind. Tell him I will see him in my rooms tomorrow morning. 9.30 will do."

"I think Mr Quarles wants the other gentlemen to hear it, sir. He says he has some news that concerns the whole College."

"News?" said Professor Ryburgh. "Why not let him come in, Dusty?"

"It's most irregular," said the Dean.

"The young gentleman said he quite appreciated that, sir, but that the matter was most urgent."

"Very well. Let him come in."

"Thank you, sir."

The five men half-turned in their chairs as Henry Quarles entered the Common Room, combining, not unattractively, an air of shyness with self-possession. He was a good looking young man in his blue coat with brass Leander buttons, a Leander tie and grey flannel trousers. All five knew and liked him.

"Well, Quarles, what is it?" said Dunton. "This is not the usual time for soliciting an interview with the Dean."

"I know, sir, and I'm sorry. But there's something I think you ought to know." He took a telegram from his pocket. "I have just heard of the sudden death of my uncle, Lord Rudham, and as he's the Patron and Visitor of the College . . ."

"Dear me," said the Dean. "This is indeed bad news. My most sincere condolences, Quarles."

"Thank you, sir," said Henry. "But please don't be sorry for me. I never liked Uncle Bob. He always snubbed me, and between you and me, sir, he was a——"

"Please!" said the Dean. "*De mortuis*, you know. I am obliged to you for the melancholy intelligence. We are officially affected, as you are no doubt aware. How did he meet his death?"

"I don't think he did meet it, sir. I gather it sprang upon him from behind. He was killed by a lion, sir."

"What a shocking thing," said Dunton.

"Most untoward," said the Professor.

"Exactly, sir," said Henry.

"Do you know what the funeral arrangements are?" asked the Dean. "The College must, of course, be represented."

"I think the funeral's over, sir. It seems that the lion ate him."

"Very dreadful indeed."

"Yes, sir. But the point is, that I am now the Patron and Visitor of the College, and I thought perhaps——"

"You are? Do you succeed your uncle, Quarles?"

"Rudham, sir. Yes, sir. Uncle Bob never had any children, not at least on the right side of the——"

"Thank you, Rudham."

"And what I thought was—it was just an idea, sir—that perhaps the College would like to take this chance of making history."

"History?" said the Dean.

"Considering the difficulty you seem to have, Rudham," put in the Professor, "to judge from your recent essays, in grasping such history as exists, are you quite sure that you want to make any more?"

"This wouldn't be dates, sir. It would be the first time that the Patron and Visitor of a College had ever stroked the College boat, and, who knows, might even go Head of the River."

"Hear, hear!" said Heseltine.

"That settles it, surely?" said Pratt.

"I am afraid I can see no change in the position," said Dunton. "If, as seems probable, you were already Patron and Visitor at the time you committed an inexcusable assault upon the College Bursar, it aggravates, not mitigates, the offence. The higher your status, the more disgraceful your conduct."

"But can a College send down its Patron?" asked Henry.

"If he is *in statu pupillari*, yes," said the Dean.

"Then that's that, sir," said Henry.

"I'm afraid it is," said the Dean. "Good night to you, Rudham. You will appear before the College Meeting at ten o'clock tomorrow morning."

"Yes, sir. Good night, sir."

Henry withdrew.

Heseltine and Pratt, with the approval of the older men, went straight to the Bursar's rooms, to make one more appeal to him. But Trout took Dunton's view—or rather the view that Dunton had thought fit to pretend to in Henry's presence—that an assault by a Patron was more insufferable than one committed by an undergraduate. Henry must go, or he would go.

That night Henry, for the first time in his life, spent an hour or two awake. He then made up his mind and slept like a top.

Next morning, a few minutes before ten, Henry, in a sub-fusc suit and wearing cap and gown, was waiting outside the Senior Common Room for a summons from the assembled Fellows. On the stroke of ten, Stibbard appeared, as noiselessly as usual.

"The Dean's compliments, my Lord, and he requests your attendance."

Stibbard opened the door and Henry marched in. There was no attractive shyness about him now; he held his head high, he was all self-confidence.

A long table had been set down in the middle of the room. At the head sat Dunton, facing the door. The Fellows, at nearly full strength, were ranged on either side of the table. Trout was there, apparently admiring the delicate mouldings of the cornice.

Henry, to the surprise of the dons who knew his customary good manners, did not wait for the Dean to ask him to be seated, but went straight to the chairs at the end of the table next to the door. He seated himself comfortably, took a paper from his breast pocket and laid it upon the table before him. And while Dunton was clearing his throat, he began to speak.

"Mr Dean and Fellows of Quarles," he began, "I have an important announcement to make to you. By this document, signed and sealed in the presence of a witness, I, as hereditary Patron of the College, have appointed myself to be your Warden. I am of Founder's Kin, I am of age, and I can read and write. This end of the table is now the head of it, and I am presiding at this meeting. What is the business, Mr Dean?"

To say that the dons were taken aback would be an under-statement. They were flabbergasted. You could not, owing to the thickness of the carpet, have heard a pin drop, but the silence was absolute. All eyes were turned to, Trout's eyes goggled at, the Dean.

With an effort, Dunton collected himself.

"Is this a joke, Lord Rudham?"

"Certainly not, Dunton."

"Do you seriously consider that you, a young man *in statu pupillari*, are a fit person to be Warden of this College?"

"I have given a lot of thought to that. Last night in bed. And the answer is yes. It will keep me steady and give me an occupation, besides making history on the river. Just think of a Head going Head!"

"Have you given no thought to the welfare of the College?"

"A great deal of thought. With a Dean like yourself, Dunton, with dons like these, with the most admirable of Bursars (he waved graciously towards Trout), what could possibly happen to upset the College's welfare? I shan't think of interfering with the teaching or the business of the College. But if, as I have heard you yourself say, a Warden should keep in touch with the undergraduates, who could better keep in touch with them than one of themselves?"

"Then you intend to stay up and take—or endeavour to take—your degree?"

"Most certainly, I do. It looks better, don't you think, for the Head of a College to have a degree, and be able to wear a gown and hood?"

"All the same," said Dunton, "I ask you, very seriously, to think again. There is a most distinguished cousin of your own, of our Founder's kin, Dr Angus McGregor. He is, by age, experience and talents, entirely suitable to be the Head of this or any other College. We have every reason to believe that it was your late uncle's intention, had he lived, to appoint him. His appointment would be applauded, not only by us, but by the world at large. Whereas yours—you must forgive me for speaking plainly—is, I fear, likely to make us a laughing-stock."

"I'm afraid Cousin Angus must take his turn," said Henry.

88

"I'm not likely to be here for life. For one thing, the Warden, by the Founder's Statute, has to be celibate. I doubt if I'm cut out for that. And as for the College being a laughing-stock, what can be nicer than to feel that one is adding to the gaiety of nations?"

"And what if this meeting votes to send you down, Lord Rudham? It is the first item on the agenda, in fact the only one."

"I am in the chair now," said Henry, "and I shall not put it to the vote. Instead, I now declare the meeting closed. I should like to add that I do not intend, for the present, to move into the Warden's Lodgings. I shall keep my present rooms on No. 14 staircase. And I hope, gentlemen, that you will all feel that you can come to me at any time with your problems. But not, unless they are very urgent, until the Bumping-races are over. Thank you. I think that is all."

And Henry picked up his mortar-board and strode, looking every inch a Warden, out of the room.

The hubbub in the Senior Common Room, after Henry's departure, was confused and confusing. The College Statute was sent for, the Peerage was sent for, coffee was sent for, the Vice-Chancellor was all but sent for, until it was remembered that in an affair of this sort the University had no standing whatever. No comfort was to be had from either *Debrett* or the Church-Latin of the Statute, and only a little from the coffee. What finally caused the Fellows to emerge into the quadrangle was the sound of cheering in the Porter's Lodge. Most unusual at this hour in the morning. An ever thickening swarm of undergraduates was milling in front of a large, bold notice, pinned to the green baize board in the porch, announcing Henry's appointment as Warden. It was, however unacceptably, clear to the dons that the new Warden was a popular choice in the eyes of the young men. The rest of Eights Week was spent, by the low-spirited Fellows, in a state of chronic dismay. Henry was a quick worker when he chose, and the announcement that Lord Rudham was the new Warden of

Quarles had appeared in the London evening papers on the day of the College Meeting. "Baby Warden for Oxford College" had been one headline, and the dons did not at all enjoy the hilarious congratulations from their opposite numbers, from the House, from Balliol, from Magdalen, from Teddy Hall. But Henry had been a true prophet in one respect. The sight of a Warden stroking his College Eight had increased the crowds, and the excitement, on the barges and the towpaths alike. And on the final night, when Quarles bumped Magdalen opposite their own barge, to go Head of the River, even T. B. Trout, disguised by dark glasses, was peeping from the anonymous swirl of spectators on the further side of the river. That he was resigned to not resigning would be to put it too strongly, but Henry's flattery and deference, whenever they met, had had its effect.

Throughout the week Henry, being in strict training, had dined apart with the Eight, and not with "the dons and the daïs serene" (or, in this case, unserene); nor had he entered the Senior Common Room. But he had attended daily in the Warden's Office on the ground floor of the Lodgings, to read and sign various routine papers, and had been declared to be a "pet" by the Lady Secretary, to his great disgust when the unwardenlike epithet was repeated to him. To his friends and fellow-undergraduates he had explained, with genuine reluctance, that, when in cap and gown, he must be addressed as "Mr Warden" and "Sir," and that certain Falstaffian familiarities and nicknames could no longer be permitted. He always addressed the Dean as Dunton. He was dignified, circumspect, and attended his lectures and tutorials. By the night of his triumph on the river Henry's position was becoming, even in the eyes of the Fellows, more improbable than impossible. Then came the Bump Supper.

It must be remembered that no Quarles boat had ever before rowed Head of the River. It must be remembered that the Warden of the College had stroked that boat. To those who remember those two points, it will be no surprise that the Bump Supper itself always has been, and always will be, remembered.

The morning after was a very beautiful summer morning. Never could the Big Quad of Quarles have looked more gracious and serene in the early sunshine, had it not been for the broken glass which lay shimmering beneath every lamp-post and about half the windows. And for the great black patch, piled high with the still smoking remnants of charred tables and chairs, which spread, in a huge irregular circle, in the middle of the trampled and disfigured lawn. And although an army of Scouts had swept up the glass by seven o'clock, and removed in wheel-barrows the bulk of the burnt debris by eight o'clock, the College remained strangely quiet. Not a man attended the roll-call in the porch at half-past seven. The Chaplain read Matins to himself and a couple of the Fellows at eight. The dons began to stroll towards breakfast in the Senior Common Room at a quarter to nine. But no undergraduate made an appearance. They were, to a man, sleeping it off.

At a quarter to ten, however, the Warden was sitting alone at the head of the long table in the Senior Common Room. He was dressed in a dark suit and a Commoner's gown; his face was pale and unshaven, and he leant his head wearily upon one elbow as he contemplated a sheet of foolscap, covered with his own handwriting, which lay on the table before him. He had, an hour earlier, by the Oxford means of scraps of white paper left by the College messenger on the corners of the Fellows' table-cloths, summoned an emergency College Meeting for ten o'clock. Stibbard was flitting about the room, laying blotting paper, ink, pens and writing-pads in front of each empty chair.

"Stibbard."

"My lord?"

"I'm afraid I must have been a bit drunk last night—wasn't I?"

"Drunk as a lord, my lord. Beg pardon, my lord."

"I wish I could remember. It's this bloody head of mine. Did I make a speech at the Bump Supper?"

"Oh yes, my lord. Two speeches—one as Warden, and one as stroke of the College boat, my lord. They were, if I may say so, exceptionally well received."

"You don't remember what I said, I suppose?"

"Not the *ipsissima verba,* perhaps, but the gist I shall always remember, my lord. I must admit that your lordship's second speech, returning thanks on behalf of the crew, was a trifle daycoozoo, to borrow a French expression, my lord."

"It's what I said as Warden that worries me, Stibbard. Was it dignified?"

"I should rather say affable, my lord. It struck a very friendly note, very friendly indeed. But I've had a word with the College servants this morning, my lord. There'll be no permanent harm done."

"What d'you mean—harm? If it was friendly?"

"Well, my lord, I think the Bursar took the view that the new rates of pay you adumbrated—not to say promised, my lord—coupled with the new hours of work, would stretch the resources of the College to an unjustifiable extent, my lord."

"Was the Bursar there? Were all the dons there?"

"Oh yes, my lord. You spoke from the High Table as Warden, if you recollect, my lord."

"But I don't recollect! That's the devil of it. Oh, blast this head! How did the dons take it? You said 'well received' just now."

"I had in mind the majority, my lord—that is to say, the young gentlemen. The Dean and Fellows were perhaps a little aloof, if you understand me, my lord."

"I didn't insult any of the dons, did I?"

"Oh no, my lord. On the contrary, your references to them were extremely cordial—Christian names, nicknames, and what I believe are called endearments, my lord."

"Good lor'! I didn't call the Dean 'Dusty,' did I?"

"Only just at first, my lord, before you had warmed up, so to speak."

"Oh gosh! And when I had warmed up?'

"I would rather not particularise, my lord. I think 'endearments' covers the case in point."

"Did the Dean seem very much——?"

"A little unresponsive, I'm afraid, my lord. Mr Dunton is rather a shy gentleman, as you know. Unaccustomed to public embraces if you follow me, my lord."

Henry groaned aloud. "Oh, my God! It's coming back to me. That bloody menace Shakespeare. Why can't I get tight without spouting him?"

"Very pretty in itself, my lord. 'Then come kiss me, sweet and twenty'—but the Dean must be nearer fifty, my lord."

"I swear he didn't look it, in the light of that bonfire. Stibbard!"

"My lord?"

"The bonfire—somebody's trousers were burnt—I don't think I burnt them—I only took them off somebody—I never meant them to be burnt—they weren't the Dean's trousers, were they?"

"Oh no, my lord."

"Thank God for that."

"Only Professor Ryburgh's. He has other pairs, of course."

"Gosh! Poor old D.B. I wouldn't have debagged him for the world if I had been sober. I swear I wouldn't, Stibbard."

"I feel certain of that, my lord."

"Not for the world. It's never even crossed my mind. Was there anything else I ought to know about, Stibbard?"

"There were a few minor incidents, so to speak, my lord. You might care to say a word to the Reverend Banner. He was looking a little bit nipped, this morning."

"How do you mean, nipped?"

"Pinched, my lord."

"The Holy Banner always looks pinched. He's so dashed ascetic."

"But this time it was lobsters, my lord."

"I can't have *made* him eat lobster—absurd."

"Oh no, my lord. It was the other way about. Live lobsters,

in his bed, my lord. I happened to see your lordship carrying a pair—exceptionally fine specimens, if I may say so, my lord."

"I remember now! But these were for Mr Barsham's bed, not for the Banner's."

"Oh no, my lord. Mr Barsham had the bullock's head on his pillow, if you recollect, my lord."

"I've told you, I recollect nothing. By Jove, yes, I do, all the same—the way those bullock's eyes looked at you! I bet Mr Barsham had fits!"

"I think Mr Barsham was more angry than frightened, my lord, to judge from a few remarks he let drop."

"Is there anybody else I must apologise to?"

"I think not, my lord. Unless you felt like a word to the Bursar, my lord."

Henry groaned again. "I don't *feel* like a word to anybody, if you really want to know, Stibbard."

But Stibbard was now at the door, for the College clock was striking ten, and a bunch of dons, all in cap and gown, were advancing purposefully across the new-mown grass. Henry rose to his feet, swaying slightly, as the Dean led them into the room. Their aspect was uniformly forbidding. Even Heseltine, even Pratt, both young enough to condone excesses of which they themselves had once been guilty, were looking serious. For they, in their wilder age, had not been Wardens.

Henry ducked his head in an attempt at a bow, but the Dean, as he seated himself at the opposite end of the table, made no response. Professor Ryburgh's usually kind grey eyes no longer looked kind. Mr Barsham was frowning. T. B. Trout looked as he had looked when taken in a landing-net, only more so.

When all were seated, Henry began to speak. His voice was hoarse and a little tremulous.

"Good morning, gentlemen," he said. "I am sorry I have had to summon you on such short notice, but the business is urgent. We have a quorum, I think."

He took up the sheet of foolscap that lay before him, and began to read from it.

94

"I am sorry to have to tell you that I was disgracefully drunk last night and made it worse by most scandalous behaviour in public. I should never have believed it of myself. I had always regarded myself as a man who, whatever the occasion for high spirits, would never transgress the bounds of gentlemanly behaviour. I think of what my good father, one of the most loyal members of this College, would have said, if he had been alive. (Here the Dean raised his eyes to glance at the speaker.) It is particularly painful to me—and, I have no doubt, to my colleagues here this morning—to have to say these things, because of my undoubted services to the College on the river. I should have hoped that my triumph of yesterday would not have been marred by this disgusting—yes, I repeat disgusting—sequel. I trust that my own feelings will prompt me to make suitable apologies to those of the Fellows whom I so rudely and childishly insulted. The bill for damage done will of course be added to my battels. And I shall not, I am sure, be surprised to learn that I have decided, with the concurrence of you gentlemen, to send myself down for the remainder of this term."

He laid down the sheet of foolscap.

"And now, gentlemen, it only remains for me to resign the Wardenship, for which I have shown myself to be quite unfitted. Mr Dean, will you be so good as to take the chair, pending the appointment of a new Warden. Yours is now the head of the table; this is the foot."

And Henry sat down, not without a feeling of satisfaction with his performance.

"Thank you, Rudham," said the Dean. "You have spared me a painful duty. And I would add that you have expressed yourself becomingly."

"Thank you, sir," said Henry. "You see, I tried to remember what Popham told me you said to him when you sent him down after his twenty-firster."

"I suspected as much," said the Dean. "Popham's father was

at Quarles; your own, as you seem to have forgotten, was, mis-guidedly, at the House."

"So he was, sir!" said Henry. "Stupid of me—I remembered that bit particularly because Popham said you never could have said what his father would have said." He turned to Barsham.

"And now I must apologise to you, sir, about the bullock's head. It was quite a mistake, sir. It was never meant for your pillow at all."

"A most gratifying thought," said Mr Barsham.

"And I must humbly beg pardon of you, Professor, about your trousers. I never meant them to be burnt, sir."

"To be honest with you, Rudham," said the Professor, "I resented their subtraction even more than their eventual combustion."

"The fact was, sir, I didn't know whose legs they were on. Legs with trousers on them look awfully alike, especially by bonfire light."

"I accept your apology," said the Professor, his grey eyes becoming kindly once more. "And I shall accept, even more gladly, a new pair of trousers for which you will pay."

"It will be a pleasure, sir," said Henry. "At least, if Uncle Bob has left me something, it will."

"And now, Rudham," said the Dean, "the apologies having been made and accepted——"

"There's still Mr Banner," said Henry. "I'm afraid I put live lobsters into his bed, by some curious oversight."

"I think you can count on Mr Banner's forgiveness. It is his *métier*."

"And I owe an apology to Mr Trout," said Henry, bowing towards the Bursar. "I have been told that I was much too free with the College's money."

"Much," said Trout, "but the pleasure of hearing you resign, Rudham, has more than made up for last night's despondency."

"I think that's all, then," said Henry. He turned towards the Dean. "You were saying, sir?"

"I was about to call your attention," said the Dean, "to the question of appointing a new Warden. Your last, somewhat hasty, appointment can hardly be ranked as a success. This time you will, I trust, give the matter more careful thought, and even take advice."

"I have, sir, very careful indeed—I've been thinking about it ever since breakfast, that is, since I drank up my water-jug, because I couldn't eat breakfast. And I've decided to appoint cousin Andrew."

"Angus, I hope you mean. Dr Angus McGregor."

"Sorry. Of course. That's the one. I could sign and seal it now, sir, if you like."

"Certainly," said the Dean.

Stibbard was rung for; a candle and sealing-wax were brought in, and the memorable Wardenship of the admirable Dr McGregor was inaugurated. In fact, although neither the Patron nor Fellows were then aware of it, this was the last occasion on which the obligation to appoint Founder's Kin was fulfilled. For on Dr McGregor's death, some twenty years later, it was discovered that the supply of literates of Quarles descent had run out. At any rate no replies were obtained to an advertisement published in three successive numbers of *The Times*. So Lord Rudham, verging upon middle-age, executed a deed transferring the patronage to the Fellows of Quarles.

But he retained a secret if somewhat shamefaced pride in the thought that he figured, if only for a week, in the honourable roll of Wardens of Quarles.

A Moment of Truth

Percy W. Fogg (formerly Wickham-Fogg, but he had dropped the hyphenated surname when, in his ardent youth, he had first joined the Progressive party) was walking through St James's Park on his way to the House of Commons, where the Shadow Cabinet of that party was to hold a routine meeting. His thoughts were as gloomy as the weather. For eleven successive years the Progressive party had been in opposition; and for the last seven of these Percy Fogg had been its leader. Intellectual and idealistic, he had gone into politics with the highest motives, at a time when the Progressives, having overwhelmed the Nationals at the polls, were full of self-confidence and reforming zeal, and very much enjoying themselves. His ability and loyalty soon brought him promotion, and he was already an Under-Secretary of State when, to his shocked surprise, an ungrateful electorate, replete with Welfare, turned round and unseated his party, though not himself, in favour of the Nationals. His venerated leaders, out of office, seemed somehow less venerable; they began to bicker, to take umbrage or life-peerages or both, and it was not long before Fogg, with his pleasant, conciliatory manners, his intelligence and his high principles, found himself the Progressives' Leader.

For a year or two he had swum along contentedly enough, waiting for the proverbial swing of the pendulum. But the pendulum had refused to swing. Against all precedent, the electorate had four times returned a Government which, in the opinion of Fogg and his friends, was wholly undeserving of the nation's confidence.

And on this dull spring morning, when the House was about to reassemble after the Easter recess, Fogg's meditations were sombre. Wherever he looked, he could find no cause for comfort.

In foreign affairs things were getting better, not worse. Since old "Mr K." and middle-aged President Kennedy had both become converts to Moral Rearmament (and rumour had it that the Prime Minister, Mr Gladwyn-Boyd, and General de Gaulle might be going the same way) there had been a definite *détente*. An agreement to scrap all obsolete weapons had already been signed; an argeement which even Russia might conceivably implement. The Aldermaston marchers, having at last woken up to the fact that Russia also possessed nuclear weapons, had travelled *en masse* to march to Moscow, since when nothing more had been heard of them. Berlin was being moved, stone by stone, into the middle of Western Germany, by the combined efforts of the Ford and Rockefeller Foundations. The prestige of the United States who had, single-handed, repulsed an invasion by Cuba, and put Marilyn Monroe into permanent orbit, had seldom been higher. Laos had changed its name to Maos, and was now as quiet as its familiar namesake.

In Africa the winds of change had taken a new and beneficent turn. This was mainly due to the invention by I.C.I. of an indelible dye with which so-called white, but in fact blotchy pinkish-yellow, people could assume a most becoming chocolate skin. Magnanimously headed by Sir Roy Welensky, the settlers in the Rhodesias and Kenya alike had taken on the new colour, causing an immediate improvement in their relations with the Africans. In Kenya, indeed, Sir Jomo Kenyatta, the Governor, was rapidly becoming to the once pink-and-yellow, now a warm chocolate, settlers what Disraeli had been to the farmers of Buckinghamshire. Even Mr M'Boya had

turned into a mellow old m'boy. The Congo was being success-
fully run by a civil service of dyed Belgians.

At home betting-shops were booming. Royalty was booming, the Queen having lately won both the Two Thousand and
One Thousand Guineas. Delinquency, according to the Home
Secretary, was deliquescent. Unemployment was depressingly
small. Steel output was deplorably large. Gold reserves (if they
were really there—who checked them? he must ask a Question
about that) were alarmingly high. The pound was looking the
dollar, and even the mark, straight in the face, dash it. The
figures for slum-clearance and new housing were disgustingly
satisfactory. At this point in his reflections Fogg suddenly
stopped, in the very middle of the bridge over the lake. He
stopped partly from shock at the words "disgustingly satisfactory" which, though not spoken, had entered his mind as
if sure of a welcome; partly because at that moment the sun
had sent a shaft of light through a rift in the clouds, illuminat-
ing the lake, the island and the pelicans, causing the stones of
the Horse Guards to shine white through the trees, and the
trees themselves to be touched with a startling brightness.
Fogg, who was sensitive to beauty, turned and gazed at the
fleeting splendour. It lasted but a moment, a moment in which,
however, he had time to note the white and yellow flash of a
pelican on his rock, hunched, full-fed, disreputable—"disgustingly satisfied" thought Fogg. And the last phrase which had
so brazenly entered his thoughts, that unspoken comment on
the Government's record in home-building and slum-clearing:
"disgustingly satisfactory" returned to him with an almost
sickening impact. What had been a moment of glory to the
lake and to the trees, had been a moment of truth to Fogg.

He felt quite shaken by his self-discovery. He crossed the
bridge and sat on a seat beneath a great plane. And recalling,
one by one, his late resentful meditations on the state of affairs
in his own country and in the world at large, he recognised with
horror that he had been sorry, not glad, when things were
going well. Good had become his evil.

He threw his mind back to the early days of his political career, to his youthful ardour and patriotism. How low had he sunk! How deeply had the long years of opposition, of disappointment, of frustration corroded his integrity! And what about his friends, his party? They, too, had been taking, as a matter of course, good news for bad, and had rejoiced at nothing but such mistakes or mischances as could be used as sticks to belabour the Governing dog. He felt deeply ashamed of himself and of them. Fogg was not without courage. He determined, then and there, to denounce himself and his colleagues at the meeting of the Shadow Cabinet to which he was now on his way. He would tell them that the party, so far as they, its leaders, were concerned, had lost its soul. They must go, and make way for new and uncorrupted men.

He rose from his seat and walked on, with an odd feeling of cleanliness. His sudden apprehension of the truth had been so clear-cut that he had no doubts but that his colleagues would see it as distinctly as himself. He had only to put it to them.

The meeting was held in one of those disproportionately lofty, dingy, Gothic apartments with which the interior of the Palace of Westminster lowers the spirits of those who have been exhilarated by its majestic exterior. Fogg, having lingered on that park seat, found most of his colleagues awaiting him. He looked at their gloomy faces, their lack-lustre eyes, with disrelish. His own step on entering had been springy, his expression cheerful. He apologised chirpily for his lateness, seated himself at the head of the long table, and immediately began to speak.

He did not describe his experience in St James's Park, preferring his audience to suppose that he had seen the light after more prolonged meditation during the recess. But he spared neither them nor himself. He was eloquent, caustic, and moving.

When he ceased speaking, there was silence, and he realised that his words had gone home.

The first comment came from Herbert Close, of the T.U.C., who remembered, even in emotion, to drop his aitches.

"You've 'it me 'ard, Percy," he said.

Albert Wigan, the once-stormy miners' leader, groaned aloud.

"Och aye," he muttered.

Henry Crabbett, the doctrinaire economist, whose ambition it was to supplant Fogg, looked round like a trapped animal. He could not, at the moment, think of an answer likely to do him any good.

Only Lady Pensteven appeared as serene, as unruffled as ever. This celebrated and high-minded woman, whose clear and beautiful phrasing of the loftiest principles had for ten years made the Commons, for five years the Lords, feel small, was quite unperturbed by her leader's condemnation. When she rose to speak, they all knew what she was going to say; they all knew that her matter would be too bright and good for their natures' daily food; but they settled themselves to listen to her without impatience, for the sheer enjoyment of that emollient voice, that crisp articulation, that incisive rhetoric. Her theme, as always, was that what mattered in a Government was not whether its methods were wise or foolish, beneficial or noxious, but the character and the motives of the men in power. To her it was axiomatic that Nationals were bad people and Progressives good people; that the motives of the former were invariably selfish, of the latter unselfish; that the acceptance of such good things as housing and slum-clearance from a National ministry was the acceptance of a bribe; and that to be content while Mr Gladwyn-Boyd was in power was to compound with the devil. When she had finished speaking, Ben Cohen, who sat by her side, and was the only member of the Shadow Cabinet except Percy himself to call her by her Christian name, said:

"While you were speaking, Rosie, I agreed, as usual, with everything you said. But now, also as usual, I don't. I am with Percy."

Ben Cohen had always been ready to pay almost any price for a gesture, and the gesture now proposed by his leader struck him as being superb.

A bitter pill, to be tolerable, must be swallowed quickly, and quickly Fogg's colleagues swallowed this one. In no time they found themselves discussing the method, and the words, whereby to announce and explain their unprecedented resolve to the Party and the public. And where were their successors to be found? Must the most promising back-benchers be interrogated, man by man, as to whether they were glad when things went well, even under a National Government, and sorry when they went badly? Might not the prospect of sudden promotion tempt not a few to be less than frank in their replies? It was all very ticklish. Soon every man at the table was busy scrawling draft announcements on the writing-pad before him, and Fogg was about to suggest the appointment of a small drafting committee, when through the door came one of those elegant figures in evening dress who lend so much dignity to the lobbies of the Houses of Parliament. He held in his hand a piece of paper, which he proffered, with a slight bow, to Percy Fogg.

Percy took it and read it. A fleeting look of astonishment turned to one of joyous excitement. He sprang to his feet, waving the piece of paper.

"My God," he said, "we've won back Bunchester. Majority three thousand eight hundred and seventy-two. And the National vote down by over two thousand! It's the turn of the tide!"

A win at the Bunchester by-election had been regarded as so unlikely that half those present had forgotten that the poll was to be declared that day. They rose to their feet as one man, waving their writing-pads in the air. Their cheering could be, and was, heard with much distaste in the Whips' room. Fogg's moment of truth was over and gone, even more suddenly than it had arrived.

The Goat

I WAS passing Mr Wix the Sexton's cottage and, having been told in the village that Mrs Wix was "a pore thing," I called in to enquire.

Mrs Wix was sitting by the table shelling peas, and I, forgetting yet once again that in these parts "better" means "well," I said: "I'm glad to see that you're better, Mrs Wix."

"No," said Mrs Wix, "I'm not better, but I'm improvin'."

"What was the matter with you?" I asked.

"Well, I can't ezackla say. But Doctor Gibbons when Wix goo for him arter I couldn't hardla touch my wittles along o' what that done to me, he say to me, 'Mrs Wix,' he say, 'the howl of your constitootion hev gone into your little finger,' he say. 'Then I hoop that 'ont goo no farther,' I say. 'Not if you dew as I tell you that 'ont,' he say. 'Dew yew keep that well iled and don't goo a-messin' about with that,' he say, 'and that'll come roight.' And that dew improve."

I said how glad I was, and we had begun on the weather, which had been ever so onseasonable, when Wix himself came in.

"He've been a-buryin' the widder Abbs," explained his wife.

"Abbs?" I said. "Do you mean the old lady down on the common? I thought she died a year or so ago." (It was some time since I had been in the neighbourhood of Hamthorpe.)

"Well, yes," said Mrs Wix politely, "but she got over that, yew see."

"They war a long-livin' lot, them Abbses," put in Mr Wix.

"Where does she lay?" asked his wife.

"I put her roight a-top of her ole man," said Mr Wix with a chuckle.

"Yew never!" said Mrs Wix. "He 'ont loike that, I don't think. They never hardla spook atween theirselves for thutty years, so I've hard tell."

"He 'ont fare to take no notice," said Mr Wix. "Besoides— that come a howl lot cheaper. 'Also Sarah, wife of the above.' There's no manner o' use in paying for a brace o' lovin' memories when one'll dew, is there now?"

"Won't she lay too shaller?" asked his wife.

"Not she. I allus puts 'em deep when there's more to come," said Mr Wix.

"You're a thoughtful man, Wix," I said.

"Yes," he said, "I am. An' I cudn't help a-laffin' to moyself arter we laid the pore ole lady to rest, when I come to think back to the toime she won that there billa-goat o' Dimmock's in the chuch raffle. D'yew moind that, Alma?"

Mrs Wix began to shake with merriment.

"That I dew," she said. "Pore old girl."

"She was allus a rum 'un," said Mr Wix.

"May I hear the story?" I said.

"Well," said Mr Wix, "that was this way. It was all along o' puttin' that there heatin' inter the chuch."

"That never hevn't heated it," put in Mrs Wix. "That's still perishin' winter-toime."

"That heat me roight enough when I'm a-stookin' it," said Mr Wix, "but that's noither hare nor thare. As I was tellin' yew, heat'un or not, that was put in, and that cost a mint o' munna, so we aimed to raise that by howldin' a Fate in the church-pightle. Rector he giv' out arter the sarmon that gifts in koind 'ud be heartla welcome from such as moight be un-awoidably prewented from attendin', an' Mrs Hedgethorne she rood on her boicycle to see them as never come to chuch. We towld her that warnt no manner o' use callin' on ole Joe Dimmock as had the small howldin' down by the moor, 'cos he'd never been known to give nuthin' away to noboda, but she never was a one to take noo for a answer, and darn me if she didn't get Joe to say he'd give one o' his goats to be raffled. So she towld him to send that up to the chuch-pightle on Saturda week, but he say No, goats was wunnerful narvous things, and he wouldn't be answerable if one o' his was to foind thatself all alown among them crowds o' people. 'Dew yew raffle for it,' he say, 'and him as wins can come here arterwards with a bit o' roop,' he say, ''cos I haint none to spare, and I'll hand that over,' he say. Well, ole Mother Abbs as lived hard by, when she hard that one o' Joe's goats was for rafflin', she towld her grandson Charlie Hipkin, him as fell off the stack harvest-toime slap onter his Dad's dinner an' got what he 'ont forget in a hurra, I'll lay—she towld him to buy her a ticket in the raffle with a sixpence what she had laid by in that ole tea-pot o' hers.

"So when Saturda week come, Charlie Hipkin fetched the sixpence and found where they was sellin' goat-tickets in the pightle and done what he'd been towld to dew and bought one o' them tickets and towld 'em to wroit 'Widder Abbs' agin the number of the ticket what he bought. When they'd sowld all the tickets and put the numbers into an old hat o' Rector's what we'd borrered of him when he warn't there, Mrs Skippon's Doris as was too young to play tricks put her hand into the hat and pulls out the fust number that come and, believe it or not, that was the Widder Abbs's number that got the goat. So Charlie run down to the Moor and tell the old lady what she been an' gone an' done and she was roight pleased and all, seein' as she allus used to say if she was to hev a nanny-goat that 'ud come very handa when she felt she cud dew with a extra sup o' milk. So she sent Charlie to borrer a roop from Baxter's and towld him to take that and goo up to Dimmock's and fetch her goat home. So Charlie come to Joe Dimmock and ax him for the prize that he promised and Joe say to him 'There-a-be—yew can hev him an' welcome,' he say.

" 'That beant a nanny-goat,' say Charlie, 'that's a billa.'

The Goat

" 'I never fared to name a nanny-goat,' said Joe. 'I towld Mrs Hedgethorne I'd give her a goat, and that's a goat roight enough.

" 'What's my granny gooin' to dew with a billa-goat?' say Charlie, 'she on't get no milk along o' him.' 'He'll be company for her, I dessay,' says Joe. 'I don't know as that'll suit her,' say Charlie. 'What'll yew give her to boy that back?' 'Boy him?' say Joe. 'He ain't wuth nawthin'. If he cud dew what he oughterer done yew don't suppose I'd a offered him to no raffle, dew yew?'

" 'I'll hev to see my granny,' say Charlie, 'afore I take him.' 'It's as yew loike,' say Joe, 'but he 'ont be hare tomorrer, not ever he 'ont.'

"So Charlie run back to his granny an' tell her what Joe done. Nat'rally the ole lady warn't pleased, but she didn't take on as Charlie thought she'd a done.

" 'Goo yew and fetch that home,' she say, 'I won that and I'm a-goon' to hev that,' she say, so Charlie fetch the ole billa-goat and hitch that up in the widder's bit o' yard. The ole billa warn't a picture, pore ole fella, but she didn't misloike him, she towl Charlie, seein' as she never won nawthin' afore and she'd allus liked them yaller eyes they hev. Well o' course Charlie Hipkin went back to his and didn't howld his tongue, and in no toime the little game Joe Dimmock played was beknownst all over the village.

"So arter we finished our teas some o' us young chaps went down to the Widder Abbs' to see her billa-goat and to hev a bit o' fun with the ole lady. But when we got to hers we cudn't see no goat nowhere. So we knocked on her door, and when she opened that we tell her we want to see the nanny-goat she won in the raffle.

" 'That ain't a nanny,' she say, 'that's a billa, as well yew know.'

" 'A billa, mother!' we say. 'What manner o' use'll that be to yew?'

" 'Never yew moind,' she say. 'He suit me.'

" 'Can we have a soight of him?' we ax her.

" 'Noo,' she say, 'yew can't. I've put him on one soide.' And she shut her door slam in our faces. Well, we was detarmined to see that ole billa-goat, so nex' mornin', as was Sunda mornin', we got up roight arla and went down to hers, and we peeped in her shud, and we peeped in her wash'us, but we cudn't see no soign o' no goat. So we knock on her door and arter a while she come downstairs in her petticoats and want to know the meanin' o' the distarbance in her yard on a Sunda mornin'.

" 'We come 'cos we doon't believe yew got no billa-goat, mother,' we say.

" 'I got him roight enough,' she say.

" 'Then whoy not let us have a soight of him?' we say.

" 'Well,' she say, 'if you must come pesterin' me loike this I suppose I better let yew hev a peek at him,' she say. 'Goo yew upstairs,' she say, 'yew'll foind that in the bedroom.'

" 'A goat in a bedroom, mother!' we say, 'what about the smell?'

" 'Oh,' she say, 'he don't fare to moind that'."

The Obedience of Father Lascaut

"It has come," said the Bishop, "the Archbishop's letter. It is just as I feared—I mean, as I had foreseen."

The Bishop of Tremblans, that ancient Provençal town, was speaking to Father Lascaut, the junior of his two secretaries, but the one to whom he was accustomed to open his heart.

The Bishop did not actually sigh as he pushed the archiepiscopal letter across the table to the little priest, because one does not sigh, in the presence of an inferior, over the orders of a superior. But he looked depressed.

Father Lascaut picked up the letter, a short printed circular, and read it.

"His Grace is a brave man," he said.

"Why brave, Father?"

"Because, your Excellency, he is proposing to pray, in the face of the world, for something which cannot be granted. It is like praying for the safety of a man who has fallen from a balloon and is hurtling to earth. Such a one is already at the mercy of God's creation—in this case the Law of Gravity. Natural laws know nothing of mercy. If they did, they would cease to be laws."

The Archbishop's letter, it must be explained, contained a direction that, on a coming Sunday, there should be said in every church in his Province special prayers for the cessation of the "Spanish Influenza." For the time was the month of October 1918, and that lethal scourge was raging, as in most parts of Europe, among the inhabitants, whether of town, village or farm, of Southern France. And the letter further enjoined, with emphasis, that every parish priest must command his parishioners, as a matter of religious obligation, to be present at such service of intercession. The letter was precise and mandatory.

"There's another thing," continued Father Lascaut. "Isn't a crowded church the last thing you want in an epidemic?"

"The Archbishop must have considered that," said the Bishop. He reached out across the table and took back the letter. "The Archbishop is not asking me for advice, or even for my opinion, Father. He is giving me an order, and I must obey it." His voice was serious, but with a touch in it of plaintiveness rather than of severity.

"Quite so, your Excellency," said Father Lascaut. But there was a stubborn look about his mouth which the Bishop knew only too well.

"This is too important a direction to be sent to the parishes by post," said the Bishop. "Half our Curé's only open their letters once a month. You and Father Menegal must divide the diocese between you, and visit the lot. You have ten days in which to do it. Both cars will be at your disposal. Make out your plans and let me see them before you go."

"Very good, your Excellency."

"And—er—Father."

"Your Excellency?"

"There is to be no winking this time. Is that clear?"

"Me? Wink?"

"Yes, Father, you."

"Very good, your Excellency. It shall be strict obedience."

The Bishop looked hard for a wink as the little priest said "obedience," but, to his relief, could detect no sign of such a thing. When Father Lascaut had left the room his superior allowed himself, in solitude, the luxury of a sigh, for he disliked the whole plan as heartily as did his second secretary.

The two secretaries, Menegal and Lascaut, got out the map of the diocese and went over it, parish by parish. It was decided that Menegal, who was a native of the country, should undertake the northern, or inland, half, where the villages, hidden among the hills or loosely strung along the red soil of the valley of the Or, were small, scattered, and ill-served by roads, while Lascaut should be responsible for the little towns of the serrated coast-line, and the hamlets in the hinterland from which, through the trunks of pine or cork-oak, you might still get a glimpse of the sea.

On a fine October morning in Provence it is difficult to be in low spirits, even when the death-rate from influenza is rising; besides the news from the front was exhilaratingly good: one might say at long last that the war was over. So Father Lascaut, using the Bishop's car in spite of being the junior secretary, since it was judged to be too good for the rougher and stonier by-roads in Menegal's sector, set out on his mission in high feather. He enjoyed driving a car; besides, during a night of meditation as well as of sleep, he had come to terms with himself about his mission. Subject, that was, to one "check-up" that he felt bound, for good order's sake, to make, and to make it he began his day by heading, not for the coast, but for a little village, actually within the southern boundary of Menegal's district, where Father Lascaut had once been the Curé. But he had left it under a cloud, and it was not to the parsonage, but to the doctor's home, that he now drove. Having started at dawn, he found the doctor, as he had intended, still at home and drinking his morning coffee. The two men, for all the doctor's militant unbelief, were fast friends. After the exchanges of *"mon vieux,"* the exclamations and the hand-clasps, the little priest, dipping a corner of his *croissant* into his *café-au-lait,* got down to business.

"This flu is very bad with you, doctor?"

"You have only to look at me," said Dr Fougeret. "Not that I have had it myself."

And indeed it was apparent from the lines of fatigue on the doctor's country face, the dark smudges beneath his grey eyes, how short of sleep he must be.

"It's a highly infectious thing, I suppose?"

"It is more than that," said the doctor. "I have cases in the most remote and solitary spots. Shepherds' huts and foresters' lodges——"

"But you wouldn't encourage people to crowd together in buildings, would you? Theatres, for instance, or even churches?"

"If I had my way it would be forbidden by law," said the doctor.

"Do you know that the Archbishop has ordered a special service of intercession, to which all the faithful must go?"

"I heard it, but I didn't believe it," said the doctor. "His Grace is not yet insane, so far as I know."

The priest drank up his coffee. "Thank you, my friend," he said. "I mustn't keep you from your work, or stay any longer away from my own."

"Giving absolution to the dying?" said the doctor. "You must be busy, poor father."

"My work, at the moment, is not so far apart from yours," said the priest. He rose to go, but turned back from the door.

"By the way, doctor, do you people get regular reports of the progress of the epidemic?"

"Naturally," said the doctor. "We both make them and receive them every week."

"By districts, or how?"

"By parishes," said the doctor.

"Who collects them?"

"Draguignan."

"Can I get hold of them?"

"The *Medical Bulletin* costs thirty centimes," said the doctor. "But you needn't spend it. I will send you my own copies."

"For the next four weeks?"

"By all means," said the doctor.

"Thank you," said the priest, and went back to his car. He had made his "check-up," and set out for St Agave with an easy heart.

The Obedience of Father Lascaut

The four years of war had left many scars upon the face of that lesser, more intimate riviera that runs westward from St Agave to Mirabelle. Where myrtle and cistus had formerly crested the red banks of the shallow cuttings through which the coast-road ran, now all was raw, torn earth. Corduroy roads of pine-logs ran in all directions into the woods, to feed vast encampments inhabited by black troops or by prisoners of war. But a landscape of mountain and sea can stand up to more scarification than mere humans can achieve, and when Father Lascaut looked, from a turn of the road, across the bay of Grandpin to the receding capes and headlands of the coast-line, he was seeing what the Ligurians, the Romans, the Saracens and (if by chance he turned his head after landing from Elba) Napoleon the First had seen before him.

The Curé of St Agave was at home, recovering from the influenza and feeling, in consequence, depressingly unspiritual. He accepted apathetically Father Lascaut's message that he was to say special prayers in his church for the withdrawal of the influenza and was deeply grateful for the injunction to lock out his congregation. At the moment the poor man was feeling that he never wanted to see his dear flock again.

"For four Sundays running, is that clear?" asked Father Lascaut.

"Excellent! I mean, perfectly clear," said the Curé.

"I am sure we shall see good results," said Father Lascaut. The devitalised Curé, thinking his visitor to be referring to his own solitary prayers in the church, could not feel so sure. "I will do my best," he said.

All the same, when Father Lascaut had departed, he felt better. The picture looked a little brighter, with four sermons the less in it.

At Pignères things were more difficult. Not only was the Curé in rude health, but he had seen a copy of the Archbishop's circular letter in the local newspaper. He pointed out that His Grace had expressly enjoined that all the faithful must attend the Intercession Service.

"Let me see that paper," said Father Lascaut.

The Curé brought it to him.

"The carelessness of these newspapers!" said Father Lascaut. "They have omitted the key-word 'not'—our archbishop is not insane. When an infectious disease is raging, it is madness to allow people to crowd together. His Grace's purpose is to end, not to aggravate, the epidemic. He is not the man to take away with his left hand what he gives with his right."

The Curé saw his point. "I will write to the Editor," he said.

"A waste of a stamp," said Father Lascaut. "I can imagine the poor man's letter-bag after such a gaffe."

"I expect you are right," said the Curé.

"Four Sundays running," said Father Lascaut.

"Willingly," said the Curé. Even a healthy priest can appreciate a holiday.

At Allion a disconsolate priest, whose conscience had not allowed him to bury an unbaptised infant in consecrated ground, had to admit that he had no congregation, and Father Lascaut lost precious time in making notes of the case for his Bishop; but at Arcaubon the Curé was briskly co-operative, and Lascaut returned to Tremblans late in the evening, weary but satisfied. He found Father Menegal in a like condition.

"How did you get on?" asked Father Lascaut.

"Famously," said Father Menegal. "They look forward to bumper congregations. And you?"

"All most helpful."

"Good," said Father Menegal.

On the succeeding days the two untiring priests, having to go further afield, spent each night in some remote parish of their respective districts, and did not meet again until their missions were accomplished. Father Lascaut had been obliged, on several occasions, to repeat his observations on the carelessness of the press, and Father Menegal had more than once to point out to some scientifically minded parish-priest that the Good God would certainly see to it that a crowding together for

Intercession should be harmless. To think otherwise would be a culpable lack of faith.

The appointed day came and went. Both priests, as in duty bound, attended the Bishop's service in the Cathedral, which was filled to capacity, and two days later both went down with severe attacks of the influenza, from which it took them a month to recover. But Father Lascaut's resulting depression was less severe than Father Menegal's, for he was comforted and heartened by the weekly reports of the *Medical Bulletin* sent to him by his friend the doctor. For the statistics, parish by parish, showed a steady decrease in the number of cases throughout the district assigned to him; whereas, in Father Menegal's territory, a sudden and serious aggravation of the disease followed close upon the day of the "bumper congregations." Father Lascaut occupied his hours of enforced idleness in carefully tabulating these figures, with a rough sketch-map of the diocese appended, on which he coloured, with dark and light blue chalks, the places where the epidemic had increased or decreased respectively. From this it would have appeared, to an Englishman, that the whole of Father Lascaut's district was for Cambridge, all Father Menegal's for Oxford. Father Lascaut was a compassionate man, and it was impossible for him to feel triumphant at such a result. Rather it caused him much painful heart-searching. Ought he not to have, could he not have, insisted to the Bishop that the Archbishop's order must be disobeyed throughout the whole diocese? He knew Menegal too well to believe that he could in any circumstances have made him an accomplice in his own plan. It would have had to be the Bishop, or nothing. In the end, remembering the Bishop's tone at the interview when he had been given his mission, he satisfied himself that no insistence on his part could have succeeded. For the Bishop had left him in no doubt that he agreed with his secretary about the absurdity of the Archbishop's order, but had decided, with a full apprehension of the probable consequences, upon obedience.

Meanwhile the Bishop himself had been receiving some disturbing letters. Two came from parish-priests in the "Lascaut sector" enclosing letters from editors of local newspapers assuring them that there had been no error in their paper's report of the Archbishop's order. But the most disturbing was from the Archbishop's own secretary enclosing half-a-dozen complaints from laymen—or rather lay-women—in the southern half of the diocese, all to the effect that in their own parish the church had been closed on the appointed day. The Bishop's comments and explanations were asked for. So that on the earliest day permitted by the doctor, Father Lascaut was summoned to the Bishop's study.

Father Lascaut knew his old friend and superior too well not to detect, even in the preliminary greetings and enquiries about his convalescence, that some part, if not the whole, of the cat must be out of the bag. He decided to attack at once, before being put upon a defence of the canonically indefensible. Before the Bishop could get through the hummings and throat-clearings that, with so mild a man as he, always piloted a rebuke, Father Lascaut pulled from his pocket and firmly laid before the Bishop his summary, with the coloured map, of the *Medical Bulletin* reports.

"I congratulate you, your Excellency," he said, "upon the results of the Intercession. Where this sketch-map is coloured light-blue, the epidemic has steadily declined since the appointed day. Roughly half the diocese. It is true that in the northern half, coloured dark-blue, the result has been unfortunate. The actual figures are on the next page. But I am sure your Excellency will agree that, in the case of so virulent a disease as this, to have checked it in fifty per cent of your parishes is a great credit to All concerned."

By a fleeting upward glance on the word "All" Father Lascaut managed to bestow a capital "A" upon the spoken word.

"Do you include yourself in that 'All,' Father?" asked the Bishop. "I notice that the light-blue half is the one allotted to yourself."

"I necessarily played my small part," said the priest, with eyes modestly cast down.

"With the strict obedience that you promised me?"

"Better than strict, your Excellency, if you remember St Paul's saying that 'the letter killeth, but the spirit giveth life.' I obeyed, I hope, in the spirit."

"Out with it, Father. What have you been up to?" asked the Bishop.

"If your Excellency will permit," said the priest, "I should like to answer that question by a parable. A Commander-in-Chief, judging that a certain enemy fortress must be conquered at all costs, ordered one of his generals to march with his army and take it by assault. The general, after a careful reconnaissance, decided that the strength of the stronghold was such that a direct assault must inevitably fail, with heavy loss of life. He discovered, however, from a deserter that the garrison was entirely dependent for its water-supply upon an underground stream which could be obstructed at a point far from the fortress itself. His engineers blocked the stream, and in a few days the garrison was forced to capitulate. Was the general disobedient in disregarding his orders to assault? The spirit of his mission was to reduce the fortress, which he did. The letter of his orders would have killed, as St Paul put it, half his men to no purpose. I may be said, your Excellency, to have acted like that general."

"In short you told the parish priests, as from the Archbishop, to forbid their flocks to attend the Intercession Service?"

"Exactly," said Father Lascaut. "And if your Excellency will be good enough to glance at the figures for the dark-blue portion of the diocese, you will see that the letter of His Grace's order has been killing people there with a vengeance. And yet His Grace's objective was to save, not to kill."

"Your general could have explained the situation to his Commander-in-Chief and got his consent to the better plan," observed the Bishop.

"Perhaps he knew his Commander-in-Chief too well," said Father Lascaut.

"Am I the Commander-in-Chief?" asked the Bishop.

"I was thinking of the Archbishop," said Father Lascaut.

"Then you are wrong," said the Bishop. "It is I you know too well—too well to take into your confidence. And you were right. *Mea culpa.*" The Bishop took up the memorandum before him and studied both map and figures. His features became heavy with dismay. He put a forefinger on the dark-blue area of the map.

"The responsibility for this catastrophe is mine alone," he said. "I disliked that letter of the Archbishop's as much as you did, Father. I should have asked for an audience and tried to persuade His Grace to cancel such folly. Who knows, he might have listened to me. He is not a man without sense."

"And if he had not been persuaded? His Grace is very devout."

"I should have had to do what you did, Father," said the Bishop.

There are times when a man must be left to himself, and Father Lascaut withdrew. Later in the day Father Menegal made his own report on "the bumper congregations." At supper the two convalescent secretaries met for the first time since they had fallen ill. Father Menegal confided to his colleague that he thought the Bishop must be unwell. He added, with a deep sigh, the reflection that, here below, a sense of duty well done must be its own reward.

Father Lascaut has a Liqueur

IT was one of those rare occasions when Father Menegal and Father Lascaut, the secretaries of the Bishop of Tremblans, were drinking coffee together, on a little balcony of the Bishop's palace. Rare, because it was the rule for these conscientious men to rise from the table, wiping their mouths, as soon as the last mouthful had been swallowed, and to return, anything but replete, to work at their desks until midnight. But the Bishop was away on his annual two-day visit to his old parents, the only visit on which no secretary accompanied him, and by the evening of the second day the good priests had dealt with all the episcopal business that could be dispatched without reference to the Bishop himself, and were now relaxed, at peace and enjoying the mellow sunshine of an early September evening. They had even, in their holiday mood, asked for liqueurs with their coffee.

Their talk had fallen, as was becoming between priests, upon the lives of the saints. Father Lascaut, being himself of an active, practical disposition, had a special affection for St Francis of Sales, but Menegal, more simply devout, had a feeling that when ruffs came in, saints must have gone out, and that no mitred bishop could compete in sanctity with a barefooted friar. For him there was no saint to compare with St Francis of Assisi.

"So far as sheer holiness goes, of course you are right," said Lascaut, gazing across the warm brown roofs to the blunt, riven mass of Roquebrune, taking on an even deeper shade of blue as the sun declined. "Tell me, Father," he went on, "if you could have been granted the privilege of being present at one incident in St Francis's life, which would you have chosen?"

Menegal sipped his coffee and pondered for a moment. Then he smiled.

"You'll think me a simpleton," he said, "which I suppose I am. But I have always thought how much I should have enjoyed hearing St Francis preach to the birds."

Father Lascaut laughed. "It's a charming story," he said, "but don't you think a Saint chirping away—tweet, tweet, tweet—might have sounded a bit comical?"

"They may have been rooks."

"Caw—caw—caw," said Father Lascaut.

"Or wood-pigeons."

"My—toe—bleeds—Betty," said Father Lascaut.

Menegal reddened.

"We are not told that Francis spoke in the language of the birds," he said.

"Then the birds understood Italian?"

"It was a miracle either way," said Father Menegal.

"I agree. But Francis was so full of courtesy," said Father Lascaut. "Isn't it more probable that he spoke to the creatures in their own language?"

"You may be right," said Menegal. The idea, which was new to him, made him wish even more strongly that he might have been there to hear.

"From what text did he preach, do you suppose?" asked Father Lascaut.

"I have always imagined it to have been from Matthew ten twenty-nine, about not a sparrow falling to the ground without the Father."

"It probably hurt just as much. And may they not have thought two sparrows for a farthing rather undervalued?"

"Not if they were rooks," said Father Menegal.

"That is begging the question," said the other. "My own

guess is that he preached about the birds having their nests. Francis liked people to count their blessings."

"It's an idea," said Father Menegal.

"And what about his sermon to the fishes?" asked Father Lascaut. "Have you never wished you could have heard that as well?"

"Well, no," said Father Menegal. "I've often thought it was perhaps a little tactless of the saint to preach the gospel to fishes."

"You are thinking of the miraculous draught?"

"That and other passages."

"Such as the feeding of the five thousand?"

"Yes—and the piece of broiled fish that Our Lord ate after the Resurrection. There's altogether too much about fishermen and fishing in the gospels not to embarrass me if I were a fish."

"I doubt if St Francis could ever have been tactless. I think he left out the gospels when he preached to the fishes," said Father Lascaut.

"What could he have found to interest them, Father?"

"I think he told them about the early Church—how the letters of the Greek word for 'fish' stood for Our Redeemer, and how a fish became the symbol of Christianity itself. Mightn't that have encouraged them? Wouldn't they have swum away proud as pike-staffs?"

"St Francis was against pride."

"You mustn't be too literal, Father. Put yourself into a fish's shoes—I mean a fish's skin—I mean a fish's scales— wouldn't you be a better fish for knowing that you were a symbol of Christianity?"

"Can a fish be better or worse?"

"Your favourite saint must have thought so."

"*Touché*," said Father Menegal, humbly. "And now, Father, where would *you* have liked best to have been with St Francis?"

"I can answer that without further reflection," said Father Lascaut. "When the Saint shook hands—or should I say paws —with the Wolf of Gubbio. The stories we have been discussing are perhaps just legends, but the wolf is a miracle I can believe in."

"Why the wolf in particular?"

"Because the same thing happened to me," said Father Lascaut.

"You're joking, Father."

"Not at all," said Father Lascaut. "I was granted the blessing of a pious mother, and she used to read to me stories of St Francis. The Wolf of Gubbio was always my favourite. I longed to meet a wolf and to lead him home."

"You flattered yourself," said Father Menegal.

"Which of us did not, at seven years old?" said Father Lascaut. "My home was in Auvergne, but my grandfather was a *garde-champêtre* in the Ardennes, and on one occasion, when I had just turned seven, I was sent to spend a few weeks with my grandparents in their lonely forester's cottage. It was, no doubt, to lighten the household work for my mother, since I remember my displeasure at finding a new baby on my return. Before I set out my Uncle Paul remarked that there were wolves in the Ardennes. My heart leapt.

" 'Real wolves?' I asked.

" 'Yes,' he said. 'But there is nothing to be afraid of. When I say there are wolves in the Ardennes, it is like saying there are murderers in Paris. Both statements are true; but one goes to Paris with a light heart. It is the same with the Ardennes: you won't see a wolf.'

"My heart sank again.

" 'How can you be sure?' I asked.

" 'I just am sure,' he said. 'So cheer up.'

"I could not cheer up, and I must have shown it, for I heard my mother ask Uncle Paul how he could have been so foolish as to mention wolves.

" 'Wolves,' she said to me, 'are much too timid to show themselves to people.'

" 'Red Riding Hood's wasn't.'

" 'That was a fairy story.'

" 'The Wolf of Gubbio wasn't.'

" 'That was a miracle.'

"In my prayers I prayed for another miracle in the Ardennes. My prayer was granted.

"I travelled to the Ardennes in the charge of the guards on the trains. When I changed trains, I changed guards. The first guard, when I told him I was going to the Ardennes, said: 'To the wolves, then?' and I felt much encouraged. The second guard depressed me. He said the wolf had been much over-rated. He was, in effect, a cowardly, skulking character. The third guard was too busy to talk to a little boy; he had his train to attend to. So I arrived at my destination not knowing what to think.

"My grandfather met me at the station. It was mid-winter and there were patches of snow on the ground.

" 'It is wolf-cold,' he said, as he wrapped a muffler round me before we set out in his light cart behind a tall, bony horse, for his distant cottage. I thought it a good omen, but I did not dare question him about wolves. I feared a disappointing reply.

"The cottage was indeed remote, and I was asleep when we arrived there in the dark. I was given hot soup and put to bed, just conscious enough to repeat my prayers for a miracle.

"The cottage stood in a small clearing in a forest of black fir-trees. They stretched, up-hill and down-hill, in all directions. To my inexperienced eye it appeared to be ideal wolf-country. The morning was clear, sharp and frosty. My spirits rose.

"After *café-au-lait* and a rusk I asked if I might go for a walk. My grandfather had already gone upon his rounds, and my grandmother, who was busy with her pots and pans, said 'Yes. If you keep to the paths and don't go too far.'

"There were paths, covered with pine-needles, leading in many directions from the clearing. On each side of the paths the lower branches and twigs of the fir-trees, dead and brown and bristly, made a barrier which it would be uncomfortable, if not impossible, to penetrate. I chose a well-defined path which ran up-hill. It was a charming path, winding itself round boulders and rocks, and promising a surprise at every loop it made. Once I was out of earshot of the kitchen-noises made by my grandmother, there was absolute silence in the forest, but for the faint crunch of pine-needles under my feet.

"The so promising path was as good as its word. Where it straightened out after an exceptionally bold loop round a giant boulder I met a wolf coming towards me. He was about ten yards away and larger than I had expected. He was neither cowardly nor skulking, for he came on steadily, apparently unastonished. He had brown eyes, a kind of ruff of coarse hair round his neck, and carried his ears cocked. I stood still. He walked straight up to me, stopped, and lifted his right paw. I seized it in my own right hand and shook it warmly. Then I turned, and with my finger resting lightly upon his neck, we returned together down the path. I felt slightly disappointed that my grandfather would not be there to see me leading home a wolf, but looked forward to the astonished applause of my grandmother.

"She happened to come to the front door to shake out a dust-pan as we approached. She looked at us, but made no sign of either surprise or congratulation. To me she merely said 'So you're back already?' and to the wolf, 'Where have you been to, Whisky?'

"I burst into tears. My disenchantment was profound. I had never seen or heard of an Alsatian dog. Owing to the thickness of the hair on his neck I had not noticed that my wolf wore a collar. I had prayed so hard for a miracle, I had shaken hands with the animal with such certainty that my prayer had been granted; and now it turned out that, so far from subduing a wild creature, I had merely made the acquaintance of a dog, a dog named Whisky, a dog to whom my grandfather had taught the art of shaking hands."

Father Menegal raised his hand swiftly to hide a yawn.

"A sad little anecdote," he said, "but hardly what you led me to expect. We were talking of St Francis and the Wolf of Gubbio, and you told me that the same thing had happened to you, and again that you had prayed for a miracle and that it had been granted. And all it comes to is that a foolish little boy couldn't tell a wolf from a dog! And, if I may say so, a bit long in the telling for so tame a dénouement." And Father Menegal yawned again.

"Tame, yes, but a miracle all the same," said Father Lascaut.

"What miracle?" said Father Menegal, with a touch of impatience.

"The dog," said Father Lascaut. "Of course I was too young and simple to appreciate it at the time. But I see now that all dogs are miracles."

"My dear Father!" said Father Menegal.

"Just consider," said Father Lascaut. "Here is a race of animals by nature carnivorous, hunters, killers, eaters of raw flesh, lappers-up of blood. And what have they been turned into? Friends, faithful, trustworthy, affectionate, eaters of biscuits, guardians of their natural victims, baby-sitters, caretakers. If that's not miraculous, what is?"

"What about cats?" said Father Menegal.

"My dear Father!" said Father Lascaut.

"And you think St Francis turned the Wolf of Gubbio into a dog?" asked Father Menegal.

"By no means," said Father Lascaut. "I think the Wolf of Gubbio was a dog. Probably the ancestor of that same Alsatian I met in the Ardennes. We know that the animal which Francis led back with him into the town lived familiarly with the townspeople of Gubbio. He neither stole meat from butchers' shops nor killed chickens. And when he died the good burgesses erected a stone to his memory."

"A stone in memory of a dog? Whoever heard of such a thing!"

"My poor Father, you should travel to England," said Father Lascaut, "or if that is too far for you, go to Clichy. There, on an island in the river, you will find noble statues of once dear dogs."

"And Francis did no miracle at Gubbio after all?" said Father Menegal.

"He had no need to. Like myself when young, he met with one. What he did, no doubt, was to explain to the people, who had never before seen an Alsatian, that the wolflike animal was a dog and therefore, like all dogs, one of God's own miracles."

"It spoils the story, all the same," said Father Menegal. "I still prefer, and even more strongly, the miracle of preaching to the birds."

"Personally," said Father Lascaut, "were I a saint, I would rather expound the wonders of the Good God than think up a wonder of my own—and one a bit cuckoo at that."

"We are not told that he preached to cuckoos," said Father Menegal.

"Oh my dear Father," said Father Lascaut.

But by now it was dark; Roquebrune stood black against a primrose sky, and a small, chilly breeze stirred the cassocks of the two priests. It was time to go indoors.

A Cautionary Tale

IF anyone had told me, himself or his pupils, at Oxford thirty years ago, that Marcus Heseltine, that tranquil, self-controlled don, would end up, in the most precise sense, as a gambler, an addict of chance—but I must begin at the beginning.

In the middle twenties of this century, Marcus Heseltine found himself, by the accident of seniority (for he had been elected Fellow of his college when unusually young), the Senior Fellow and Tutor of Quarles. He was not much over forty, a smallish, spare man, not distinguished, but profoundly conscientious and entirely devoted to his college and his work. He taught history, without fire or inspiration, but with an affection for the past and an almost cosy familiarity with the persons who guided, or are thought to have guided, its affairs. He was reputed to be writing a life of Carteret but it has never been published.

Socially Heseltine was a quiet, kindly, serviceable man, popular with dons and undergraduates alike; he had not a great deal to say, but what he did say was sensible and to the point. Above all he was equal-minded—nobody had ever seen him excited or depressed. He took things as they came, and a thing that came was the serious illness of the Warden of Quarles, the celebrated Dr Angus McGregor. So serious was it that the Warden was ordered by his doctors to winter abroad, and Heseltine, as Senior Fellow, found himself acting as Vice-Warden for almost a year. He took over his new responsibilities without misgiving, and when, soon after his temporary promo-

127

tion, it was the turn of the Bursar, T. B. Trout, to have a sabbatical six months of absence, Heseltine, together with Pratt, the senior classical tutor, and Keech, the philosopher, was appointed by the Fellows to take charge of the Bursary. It was then that Harry Lockhart, an old pupil of Heseltine's, came down to spend a week-end with his former tutor.

Harry Lockhart was a stockbroker. In those days it was unusual for Quarles men, especially men who, like Lockhart himself, had taken a good Honours degree, to become members of the Stock Exchange. There was still, to the sensitive noses of scholars and gentlemen, a faint odour of raffishness, or, at least, of a kind of low-brow money-grubbing, about that honourable and indispensable profession. But there was nothing raffish or low-brow about Lockhart. He was highly intelligent, straightforward and hard-working. And by his not unfrequent visits to his old college and his lively talk when a guest at High Table or in the Senior Common Room, he had imperceptibly, over the years, converted the Fellows of Quarles to a juster view of stockbroking. They had heard rumours, with a half-shocked admiration, of a Cambridge college that had made a fortune through the market operations of its Bursar and, without professing openly any envy of such get-rich-quick methods, they were apt, on the occasion of Lockhart's visits, to question him, with increasing particularity, about how such operations were performed.

On this particular visit a conversation took place between Heseltine and Lockhart which got much nearer to the bone than had former ones. It took place in Heseltine's own rooms—donnish and, close to the barred brightness of the fire, even cosy—with only Keech as a listening third. So near to the bone did the talk get, that it ended in Lockhart roundly asking Heseltine the amount of the College's invested funds and how much income they produced.

Heseltine had been hoping that the question might be asked. Since taking over the Bursary from the aloof and secretive Trout, he had learnt for the first time that the College had a matter of two hundred thousand pounds in government securities, the proceeds of farmlands sold, on the occasion of the first impotent Labour Government, by Trout's predecessor, who had mistakenly foreseen the nationalisation, if not the confiscation, of all real property. The gross income was some nine thousand a year.

"I take it," said Lockhart, "that as a College you are restricted to Trustee Securities?"

"There is no Trust," said Heseltine. "We could do as we liked with our land, and I presume we can do as we like with our money. Isn't that so, Keech?"

Keech, the junior Fellow, nodded. An ardent, active young man, completely dedicated to Quarles, he had long doubted whether the close, pedantic Trout had been making the best of his stewardship.

"If that's the case," said Lockhart, "why don't you swap into equities? You can immediately increase your income by two thousand a year at the least, with excellent chances, if you choose the right securities, of eventual capital appreciation."

"Two thousand a year's not to be sneezed at," said Keech.

"But how are we to choose the right securities?" said the more cautious Heseltine.

"Leave that to me," said Lockhart. "My firm will make out a list for your consideration, with detailed reasons for our choice."

"We shall have to consult the Prattler," said Heseltine.

"Of course," said Keech.

"And get the College to sanction it."

"Naturally," said Keech.

"All right, Harry," said Heseltine. "Get out your list and we'll have a meeting on it."

"I'll come down with it myself next week," said Lockhart, "in case you have any questions."

"Thank you, my dear Harry," said Heseltine. "That will be best."

It did not turn out to be best, but Heseltine could hardly,

had he been even less simple than he was, have foreseen to what this non-committal fireside chat was in the end to lead him.

Pratt, the third member of the Bursary Commission, was at first somewhat lacking in enthusiasm for the plan; not because he had financial misgivings, but because he had not been present when it was broached. He was a fine scholar, but always a little on his dignity; it was wrong, he felt, that Keech, not he, should have been in on an affair of such moment while he himself had been excluded. But after Heseltine had assured him that it was Harry Lockhart, not he nor Keech, who had brought this matter up, his doubts were removed. On the following Saturday evening, he was not the least eager of the three to study Lockhart's list, and to listen, with occasional flashes of comprehension, to Lockhart's comments.

Heseltine himself, fortunately, had no hesitation in confessing his ignorance, and came to the aid of his two colleagues with ready questions about the nature of deferred shares and the functions of a Trust Company. They had only to nod after Lockhart's lucid explanations had been given. By the end of the session their minds were made up. At the next meeting of the Fellows they would recommend a wholesale switch from gilt-edged securities into ordinary shares.

Trout, the Bursar, was not a popular member of the Senior Common Room. A tight-lipped lawyer, inclined to pedantry and legalism, he often found it beyond him, at College meetings, to disguise his contempt for scholars, philosophers and historians when they presumed to question him on matters of business. In his rarer genial moods he treated them as children, in his habitual ones as donkeys, and they resented it. He was, as has been said, naturally secretive, disclosing to his colleagues as little of the College's affairs as he could get away with. So it was with the high spirits of mice when the cat is away that the Fellows, at the next weekly meeting, listened to Heseltine's accurate and fluent repetition of Lockhart's views and proposals. The prospect of an increased revenue was exhilarating, but that of achieving it behind Trout's back was even more exciting; and the Fellows not only authorised the triumvirate to go ahead, but warmly congratulated them on their financial flair. Lockhart was written to, and the securities sold and bought.

A few months later Trout returned, and the complacent three explained to him, in a matter-of-fact way which would, they hoped, conceal the triumph they were feeling, their transactions in his absence. Their complacency was brief. In icy, cutting tones Trout informed them that what they had done was entirely *ultra vires*. The absence of a Trust Deed was irrelevant. All funds held by a College were assumed to be held in trust, and their investment must be restricted to Trustee Securities. The operation must be immediately reversed; the equities sold and the gilt-edged repurchased; and the expenses of the former transaction, as well as any loss incurred, charged to those persons responsible for the breach of trust.

The historian, the classic, and the philosopher stood momentarily speechless. Not one of them was qualified to contradict a lawyer on a question of law. Then the equable Heseltine found his tongue.

"That is *your* opinion, Trout," he said.

"It certainly is," snapped Trout.

"In a matter of such gravity, I must ask you to get it confirmed. And by the highest authority."

Trout actually laughed; he foresaw that he was going to enjoy himself.

"By all means, my dear chap," he said. "I'll take MacQueen's opinion, if that satisfies you?"

MacQueen was a leading Chancery K.C. of whom even dons had heard.

"If MacQueen agrees with you, there's no more to be said."

"If!" said Trout.

Trout was not a man to waste time. On the following evening he returned from London with MacQueen's opinion in his pocket. At greater length, but no less roundly, it confirmed what Trout had said. The Fellows' weekly meeting, in spite of Trout's joviality, was the gloomiest in the remembrance of any Fellow present. "Breach of Trust" has an ugly sound; a sound Trout emitted, his sombre eyes bright for once, several times over.

A week later Trout informed the College meeting that the reverse transaction had been completed, and that the College, with its funds safely re-invested in government stocks, could hold up its head again. The net loss on the double operation, including stamp duty, brokerage, and a fall in the price of equities, was about £4500. The liability for this loss fell, the Bursar explained, with an attempt at casualness which failed to conceal his pleasure, upon those persons responsible for the breach of trust. It was arguable, he said, that since the Fellows as a body had sanctioned the misfeasance, the liability should be apportioned between all those present when the sanction was given. But personally he felt that, since his colleagues were none of them either lawyers or business men, the whole loss should be borne by those who had planned and initiated the deal. Men who had assumed the powers and responsibilities of the College Bursar were, in his humble view, far more culpable than the innocents whom they had led into trouble. However, Trout concluded, it was not for him to say. The Fellows must settle that between themselves. Gathering up his papers, he rose, excused himself to the presiding Fellow, Heseltine, and left the meeting. Through the great window of the Common Room, Heseltine, from his seat at the head of the table, could see the jauntiness of Trout's gait as he crossed the grass. The Bursar was all but skipping.

A silence had fallen upon the assembled Fellows, while each of them was making rapid calculations in his head. How many had been present at the fatal meeting? Twenty? That would mean £225 apiece, should they decide, as most of them gallantly attempted to decide, that all must take their share of the loss. But for some of them £225 was a sum beyond their capacity; for all of them it would be a crushing burden. For all of them, that is, except for Heseltine himself. Heseltine was the only Fellow of Quarles to have a private fortune. Without being exactly rich, he was comfortably off. They all knew this, and struggled, in their dismay, not to remember it.

Heseltine remembered it, of course. From the moment that he heard Trout announce the amount of the damage, he decided to meet it himself. It would not be convenient; it would have to be replaced, if his nephews and nieces were not to be the sufferers from his mistake, by personal sacrifices over several years. But he could pay it, and he would do so.

"Well, gentlemen," he said, "that's that. I think it concludes this morning's business. We shall have to think out the fairest solution to this little trouble."

Heseltine would dearly have liked to relieve the visible unhappiness in the faces of many of his younger colleagues by announcing there and then that he intended to take the thing upon himself. But he foresaw the result of any such announcement: the protests, the hubbub, the emphatic insistence by Pratt, by Keech, that they must and would bear their share. Things would be said in public which the sayers would be too proud to withdraw subsequently. He felt he could go no further than attempt to lighten the gloom by a reference to "this little trouble."

Naturally this did not lighten it, even increased it. "It's all very well for Heseltine to call it 'little'" was the first reaction of the younger and more penurious dons. And their heads refused to follow their hearts in the desire of those softer organs that Heseltine should not be penalised for having given a lead in a plan that all had approved. The thought that the broader shoulders of the Vice-Warden and Vice-Bursar were, after all, the proper ones to assume the burden kept on returning to them.

Had Heseltine known their thoughts, he would have been delighted. But, as it was, he had his hands full with Pratt and Keech. Singly and together, these two accomplices were instant and insistent in pressing upon him the view that the liability must be shared equally between the three of them. They had been given equal voices when the Bursary had been put into commission, and there could be no difference of degree in the responsibility of each one of them. Heseltine was learning, for the first time, how hard it can be to be generous. It was absurd, of course, that Keech, with about half Heseltine's emoluments and not a penny of capital, should be expected to take upon himself a full third of the liability. He just had not got the money. And Pratt, being a married man, was hardly better off. Yet Heseltine was confronted by the irrational stubbornness of pride, where governed by a sense of justice. His days and nights were clouded by the sense of being up against a brick wall, when he was so willing, and so well able, to settle the whole thing once and for all.

There is no knowing how long the battle with his pig-headed colleagues might have continued, had not the Warden returned, like a god in a machine, from his sick-leave. Heseltine told him the whole story. The Warden listened, puffing his pipe.

"It was bad luck," he said, when Heseltine had finished his tale, "but Trout's an ass. You can't commit a breach of trust, except in the most technical sense, if you don't know that a trust exists. In any case, when there's no *mens rea*, there's no culpability. The loss is the College's. I've no doubt that, when there's a change of Bursar, we shall soon make it up. How did the Torpids get on?"

The Warden's decision was law. The fellows breathed again, with the exception of T. B. Trout, who gasped, and of Heseltine himself. For Heseltine's conscience refused to lie down. He kept going back in his mind to his first talk with Lockhart; he remembered how he had almost willed Harry to question him about the College's funds. He had not knowingly committed a breach of trust, but he had been ambitious, as Vice-Bursar, to take the talent entrusted to him out of a napkin and to put it out to fructify. Say what the Warden might, he knew that he had, in truth, been the prime mover in the events which had cost the college these thousands of pounds.

Heseltine, for the first time in his life, became a worrier. He would never regain his serenity, he felt assured, until he had made restitution. But it must be indirect; made at a time, and in a form, that could by no possibility tie it up with an affair that the Warden had declared to be closed.

The College had no lack of wants, and, like all Colleges, would have welcomed donations from old Quarles men—or from anybody else—with which to satisfy them. But Heseltine's difficulty was that while it was well known that he had a comfortable income, it was generally understood that he regarded his capital as earmarked for those nephews and nieces of his. An offer of £5000 for the new bathrooms, or for the library extension, would be immediately recognised, coming from Heseltine, as "conscience money" and would cause renewed agonies to the austere Pratt, the quixotic Keech. For many a month Heseltine turned the thing over, but could not see his way.

In the long vacation he re-visited Venice. And, sitting in St Mark's Square, or strolling along the Riva degli Schiavoni, for the first time he found himself, as he gazed and gazed at the most triumphant achievements of Western civilisation, ceasing to take such magnificence for granted, as something "given," and pondering about the means whereby the citizens of one small city had contrived such incomparable splendours. Pride, vainglory, piety, ostentation, Hell-insurance, a passionate love of beauty—all no doubt had their share in the ends these men set out to attain, but the means? Only fearless, even reckless, speculation, a compulsive will to make money at whatever expense of lives, fortunes, peace and contentment, could have provided the means. Those men must have driven themselves, incessantly, regardless, by hook or by crook, to amass wealth.

Heseltine, the quiet don, sipping his *strega* in the sunshine and thinking such thoughts, felt himself to be a poor creature indeed. What was his own genuine, but static, dedication to his College worth beside the rushing, headlong activities of those old Venetians on behalf of their city? Bathrooms indeed! What

Quarles needed was a benefactor with the vision—and the cash—to pull down the monstrous, turreted Butterwater erection in the Back Quad and to build in its place something with the nobility, the grace, to match the serene perfection of its older courts. He began to day-dream. Walter Mitty had not yet been invented, to mock day-dreamers, and Heseltine was free to consider how men could, and did, make great fortunes. He remembered again that Cambridge college, enriched, they said, by speculation. He had his talent, his fifty thousand pounds, laid up in a napkin. As he sat there, in the Piazzetta, close to the great columns stolen from Tyre, he looked up at the Doge's Palace, he glanced left at St Mark's, he gazed across the Lagoon to San Giorgio, he looked over his right shoulder at the majestic dome of the Salute, and felt abashed. With what courage, in the face of what hazards, must the men who built these have wrapped their talents and put all to the touch! Heseltine ordered another *strega*.

In the train going home, sitting up all night in a second-class carriage because, being able to afford a first-class, he did not choose to be seen in one, Heseltine came to a decision. He would, on his way through London, consult Harry Lockhart.

Heseltine was a stranger to the City. And when, after many enquiries, he found himself in a narrow alley off Draper's Gardens, at the foot of a bare stone staircase, seeking for the name of Lockhart's firm among a score or more that crowded a great wooden panel, Heseltine had a moment's misgiving. Could one among so many, so dingily lodged, hold the key to the wealth he was out for? The appearance of the lift and the lift-man was not reassuring, any more than that of Lockhart's outer office, with ENQUIRIES written over the arched opening of a small grey cubbyhole. But, once in Lockhart's own room, Heseltine's spirits revived. Here all was comfort, warmth and light. Curtains, flowers, a couple of French Impressionist pictures, combined in reassurance. Above all Harry himself, in short black coat and sponge-bag trousers, button-holed, bright-eyed, radiated confidence from behind an enormous knee-hole desk.

"My dear Harry!"

"My dear Marcus."

Heseltine explained, with many a shy understatement, what he was after. He had this money: he wanted to treble it: he was prepared to be bold. Did Harry know of some gold-mine, some diamond-mine, some new invention, in which he might take an interest on the ground floor?

Harry laughed. Had he known, had he ever been in a position to know, of such opportunities, he would hardly be sweating away as a stockbroker. Those who knew of ground floors, and they were rare enough, kept them to themselves. But there were safer, if slower, ways of speculating. The American stock-market, for instance: at the moment it appeared to be uncommonly promising. Business was booming, and shares were booming with it. If Heseltine would care for a flutter in a biggish way in some of the market leaders in New York——

"But I've only £50,000," broke in Heseltine, "and I want £150,000: £100,000 for Quarles and £50,000 for my nephews and nieces. Surely no reputable company's shares have ever trebled in value?"

"They have, over the years," said Harry. "But I wasn't thinking of that. If you speculate, you won't be buying American shares with your fifty thousand pounds. You will buy them with far larger amounts, which you will borrow."

Heseltine was shocked. "Me borrow?" he said.

"Naturally," said Harry, "if you want to make big money. Now, listen to me."

And Harry, with his accustomed lucidity, gave to the cloistered don an exhaustive lecture on carry-overs, contangoes, margins, account-days, and the whole elaborate machinery by which a man with £50,000 can buy and sell shares in vastly greater amounts.

Heseltine had a good brain. What every stockbroker can grasp, Heseltine could grasp. And he did grasp it, with elation. He knew, for the first time in his life, what excitement meant. His dream might, after all, come true.

Harry did not fail to warn him that rising markets must eventually turn; that luck as well as watchfulness would be required, and that the results he arrived at were unlikely to be achieved for many years to come, if at all. Heseltine assured him that he had patience, which was true enough. He then asked Lockhart to promise secrecy (a request which, Harry explained, coming from anyone less innocent of affairs than a don would have been an insult) and told him to go ahead.

It would be wearisome to catalogue the Public Utilities, the Chain-stores, the Steel, the Railways, the Copper, the Motors, the Foodstuffs, the Drugs, the Transport, the Telephones, the Radio-sets, the Gramophones of which, from day to day, week to week, month to month, during the next two years, Heseltine became a temporary part-owner. It had been his luck, as a green and inexperienced speculator, to enter the game in the early days of the greatest "bull" market of the century. Thanks to Harry's vigilance, on no occasion was he called upon to find cash for a marginal loss. In his quiet rooms at Quarles, on Easter reading-parties on Dartmoor or the Lakes, on his Long Vacations abroad, his inner excitement was continuous. He himself had little to do but to say "yes" in reply to Lockhart's proposals. True, he was put to some little trouble in concealing his unaccustomed activities. Financial newspapers, dailies and weeklies, had to be scanned furtively and as furtively disposed of. Lockhart's initial practice of sending him telegrams had to be promptly forbidden. More difficult still was the problem of disguising, from his colleagues and pupils, the buoyancy of his spirits. He was by nature no actor. Attempts to appear unconcerned when his heart was singing were invariably overdone. A "Cheer up, Marcus!" or a "What's wrong, Marcus?" from some fellow-don were sure signs that Heseltine had that morning received good news from Draper's Gardens. He found it safer to make no effort, and to rely upon his past reputation for a natural cheerfulness.

None the less, the Senior Common Room did mark a change in the Senior Fellow. He who had been so adept at small talk, so generally conversable, was less on the spot than formerly. He had moments of absentmindedness, when a faraway look would come into his eye; not a look of anxiety or of serious preoccupation so much as that of a visionary. And in truth at such moments Heseltine was seeing not a castle exactly, but a college in the air, slowly taking on substance and subsiding on to familiar lawns, standing there at last, gracious, dignified, yet intimate and inhabitable.

Meanwhile, the old Warden, after a brief St Luke's summer, died. Not once did it occur either to the Senior Fellow or to his colleagues that Heseltine might be chosen to succeed him. In most professions, perhaps in most colleges, a second-in-command, upon the death of his chief, can hardly refrain from nourishing secret hopes of promotion. It was not so at Quarles. The Warden of Quarles must be a man of distinction, not necessarily in the world outside, but recognised to be head and shoulders above his fellows. And this Heseltine decidedly was not. There were some younger men—there was the dedicated Keech—who might some day make the extra growth required of a future Warden. But on this occasion it was clear that the College must look outside for its new Head.

After much discussion, it was finally agreed to elect J. P. Carstairs, Professor of Moral Philosophy at a northern university. Carstairs was an old Quarles man; at fifty-two he was in the prime of life; he was a philosopher who had made philosophy almost intelligible; he was a practical man; he had a sense of humour; he was widely known and admired. Heseltine, not seeing all his own mischance, voted for him with confidence and satisfaction. Since the vote was unanimous, Heseltine was never in a position to look back upon this vote as the most fated action of his life. Had it been a casting vote, he would undoubtedly have done so.

For a time after the new Warden's election life in Quarles jogged along much as before. The Common Room decided, quite wrongly, that Heseltine's fits of abstraction must be due to his *Life of Carteret*. The something not far from "starriness" in Heseltine's eyes could conceivably be accounted for, as a young historian pointed out, by the irrepressible good spirits of that convivial statesman. At all events, Heseltine continued with his market operations unsuspected, and concealed his unchecked elation with a discretion made perfect by practice.

By the end of the year 1928 Heseltine had made his pile. The great "bull" market, bolstered by the optimism of the great American people, had swollen the fortune of this outwardly tranquil, workaday don, to something near a hundred and fifty thousand pounds. As soon as the account arrived from Lockhart's office showing these figures, Heseltine decided that the great moment had arrived. He would announce to the College, through the Warden, his intention to make a gift of a hundred thousand pounds for the rebuilding of the Back Quad. That it would be accepted he had no doubt. In those years the reaction in favour of Butterwater had not begun (except in the mind and heart of a certain youth named Betjeman). The majority of the Fellows were used to deplore those turrets, those pepper-boxes, those bastard, stunted, lancet-windows as warmly as Heseltine himself. It was Heseltine's finest hour. He made an appointment with Carstairs. He found him relaxed and at ease in his study. There was a deep armchair for Heseltine by the fire; there was a cup of tea and a crumpet on a small table by the arm of the chair. The surroundings were propitious.

"Well?" said the Warden, when both were comfortably settled, for Heseltine had warned him that the interview had been asked for to discuss a matter of moment.

Heseltine's acquaintance with the new Warden was still superficial. The Warden, although anything but diffident, was shy; a son of the Manse, nourished on oatmeal, who had climbed, bursary by bursary, up the educational ladder, he had none of the natural ease of old Dr McGregor who, although a fellow-Scot from an impoverished family, had walked through life as if swinging a kilt. For he had been near kin to the Chief of his clan; whereas Carstairs was a Lowlander whose pride, deep as his predecessor's, was a source of stiffness, not of ease. But he had humour and kindliness, and Heseltine, during the six months or so of their acquaintance, had been afforded no occasion to detect in him the stern, implacable puritanism of the Scot turned Moral Philosopher.

So Heseltine told his story: of his dream in Venice, of his visit to Lockhart, of the "bull" market, of his triumph, of his intended munificence to the College. For a moment he thought, when he had finished his tale, that the Warden was embarrassed at the magnificence of the proffered gift. He wished he had not ended up with "a hundred thousand pounds" in quite that tone, with that rather unnecessary emphasis. Had he been—he, the dreamer—a thought vulgar?

For the Warden certainly displayed every sign of embarrassment. For one thing, he was speechless. For another, he crossed and uncrossed his legs, like a man in two minds. And he made a botch of trying to light his pipe. At last he spoke.

"It's a most generous offer, Heseltine," he said. "Most generous. But—er—but—am I right in thinking that you have been *gambling*?"

He pronounced the word gambling in the tone of contempt, almost of disgust, with which a Headmaster says "drinking" to a sixth form boy.

"I prefer 'speculating,' Warden," said Heseltine.

"It's the same thing," said Carstairs. And rising suddenly to his feet, the Warden stood over his visitor, back to the fire, and, with blazing blue eyes, lectured this ripe don, this Senior Fellow and Tutor of his College, on the evils of gambling, on the immorality of amassing wealth without working for it, that might have come straight from a pulpit. At last he made an end and sat down.

"The College could never accept it," he said.

Heseltine, aghast, angry and rebellious, stood up in turn.

"The College has not yet heard of it. Those are your private views, Warden. I must ask you to put my offer before a full College Meeting. I, of course, shall not attend."

"Certainly," said Carstairs. "The generosity of your intention entitles you to that. But I can hold out no hope. There are certain principles at stake."

"We shall see," said Heseltine.

He left the Warden's Lodging indignant, ruffled, but not in despair. His colleagues, surely, were not so entirely out of the world, so impracticably high-minded, as to reject out of hand so bountiful a windfall. Gambling indeed! You gambled with dice, with cards. What would poor Lockhart think, to hear all his watchful care, his expert discrimination, described as a gamble? No, he thought, there was no cause for depression. The Warden would be, must be, outvoted.

The Warden, guessing the Senior Tutor's misery, called an emergency meeting of the Fellows for the following morning. There was a full attendance. Carstairs informed them of Heseltine's proposed gift, and repeated to them, with scrupulous accuracy, Heseltine's own account of his dream in Venice and of his operations on the American market. There were excited murmurs of astonishment, pleasure and approval from many parts of the room. The Warden looked round the long table. His eyes began to blaze, as they had blazed at Heseltine in his study.

"Of course," he said, "it is for you to decide whether or not to accept this gift, the product of gambling. For my own part, as I have already told the Senior Tutor, I shall oppose it." And he then harangued his colleagues in much the same terms as he had lectured Heseltine, but stressing the responsibility of a College, as mentor of impressionable young men, to set an example of unassailable probity.

There was silence when he had finished.

"*Non olet pecunium*," muttered Pratt at his elbow.

"An ancient and disreputable evasion," exclaimed the Warden.

"Our sixteenth-century endowments came from robbing the Church," remarked a younger Fellow.

"This is not the sixteenth century," said the Warden.

"Supposing he had held his tongue about how he came by the money?" asked another.

"But he didn't," said the Warden.

"Of how many rich men could it be said that they never speculated?" asked somebody.

"I've no idea," said the Warden.

"What about the parable of the talents?" asked Keech.

"Trade is not gambling," said the Warden. "There is no hint that the successful servants borrowed ten times their capital in order to make their profit."

"Supposing Heseltine had inherited this fortune from an uncle, and it turned out that the uncle had made it on the turf?" asked the Junior Fellow.

"I should have regarded the gift as penance for, not the fruit of, ill-doing," said the Warden.

"Can't we regard it as Heseltine's penance for gambling?" suggested Keech.

"He couldn't be less penitent," said the Warden.

"What if we refuse it and Heseltine leaves it to the College in his will?" asked Trout's successor as Bursar.

"I refuse to contemplate the demise of our dear Marcus," said the Warden.

"A new and charming evasion," muttered Pratt.

And now the Fellows began to turn one towards the other, and to discuss it in groups. The Science Tutor was heard to say that, had the money been for laboratories, he would have been all for accepting, but since it was to destroy some of Butterwater's finest work, he was content to let it go. Heseltine's will was as hotly discussed as if, in his early forties and uncommonly hale, he were already in his grave. Two of the younger fellows nearly came to blows over the style of architecture which was to take the place of the present Back Quad.

The Warden sat, silent and patient, in his place. But when a man is, intellectually and morally, head and shoulders above the rest; when he sticks, unflinchingly, to the ethical view; when he has determination and, above all, is Warden, his advantages are enormous. Little by little the scattered discussions died out and the Warden, dominant, stubborn, and embarrassingly high-minded, returned to the charge. He made the dissidents, and they were not few, feel themselves to be worldlings, average sensual men, in the presence of integrity. It was an uncomfortable feeling. When the vote was taken, several abstained, but not a Fellow had the pluck to declare himself to be lacking in principle. Heseltine's gift, with many tributes to his generosity, was declined by the College.

The collapse of his dream was a shattering blow to Heseltine. But the reason given for the refusal of his gift was, to a man so sensitive as he, still harder to bear. He decided, without hesitation, that he must resign his Fellowship. How could a man condemned by his colleagues for unethical behaviour continue as an instructor of youth?

Oddly enough, the Senior Tutor's resignation took both Warden and Fellows by surprise. The Warden, like many Puritans, was at heart a most tolerant man: he did not expect everybody to live up to his own strict standards. In denouncing "gambling" and refusing the benefaction he had been concerned with himself and his principles; not for a moment had he thought of his friend Marcus as being unfit to be a Fellow. The other dons, left to themselves, would probably have accepted the gift without misgiving, even with a sneaking admiration for the unsuspected dash and adventurousness of their quiet colleague. They had, without fully realising it, been overawed by the Warden's imposing scrupulosity.

Naturally his friends tried to persuade him to change his mind. The worldlings among them told him that his good influence over his pupils would be enhanced, not diminished, should they ever learn that their tutor was a sportsman and a lucky one. Even the Warden begged him not to take things so much to heart. But it was of no avail. Heseltine's resignation was formally made and had to be accepted.

But it did not occur to him to leave Oxford and the surroundings, physical and human, in which alone he felt at home.

He took comfortable rooms in Beaumont Street, talked vaguely of coaching, and returned to his notes on Carteret.

In the middle of this uprooting Heseltine received a letter from Lockhart, to whom he had not so far had the heart to confess the end of his dream. Harry advised him to close his market operations. The great "bull" market might yet run for months, or even a year, but Harry found signs, here and there, that the thing had been overdone. Nobody could hope to get out at the very top of a market. Marcus had made a fortune; he should, said Harry, cash in on his American equities and return to gilt-edged.

Heseltine did not answer the letter. For one thing his heart was too sore to think about a fortune for which he had, now, no use; for another, still subconscious reason, he was reluctant to abandon a pursuit which, through habit, had become almost necessary to him. His life would lose, he felt without quite acknowledging it even to himself, a good deal of its charm without the daily perusal of his financial papers, the scanning of market-prices, the satisfaction in watching his various holdings go up and up.

The truth was, of course, that the Warden had been right. Heseltine had become a gambler. For all his vision of a splendid purpose, he had for some time now been enjoying the game for its own sake, and Lockhart's warning had in fact, although Heseltine was slow to acknowledge it, added an attraction to the game. It had introduced a not unpleasant spice of danger.

After about six weeks Lockhart wrote again. The signs of a crack in the market were increasing, he said. He no longer advised, he begged his client to close his speculations. So far his gains were unimpaired, but a change might come any day, and without warning.

Heseltine answered this letter. He told Harry the whole sad story of the College's refusal of his proffered gift and of his resignation. Since the amount of his fortune no longer mattered, whereas the amusement he got from speculation was considerable, he would go on for the time being.

Lockhart replied that in that case he could no longer make any proposals or take any responsibility. Heseltine must operate off his own bat, and take the consequences.

Heseltine felt the exhilaration of a deerstalker when the professional stalker for the first time tells him to stalk his own stag. He no longer regarded himself as an amateur. He had been watching the American stock-market for three years, and felt his judgment to be as good as another's. He acquired a thick sheaf of telegram-forms, and spent twice as much time as before on reading the financial papers, and half as much on Carteret. He enjoyed himself immensely. When the sudden and overwhelming collapse of the American market took place; when stockbrokers, and even bankers, were falling from sky-scrapers with not much less frequency and about the same thuds as lumps of snow off a glass roof, Heseltine, like wiser men than himself, was caught out. It was no good telegraphing "sell," for there were no buyers. In a couple of days the whole of Heseltine's profit of a hundred thousand pounds was wiped out, and only Lockhart's prudence in insisting on a proportion of tough, panic-resisting securities saved for those nephews and nieces of his the original fifty thousand pounds. He could regard himself as a very lucky man.

To his losses he was quite indifferent, but the blow to his self-esteem was, momentarily, a sharp one. The very magnitude of the disaster, however, carried consolation. He had been an ass, but among a very multitude of other donkeys.

All the same, Heseltine found it hard to recover his spirits. Even the admirable, ebullient Carteret failed to succour him in his depression. He was like a smoker who had given up smoking: for ever fidgeting, restless, and ridden by an unsatisfied craving. But a smoker knows exactly what he wants, whereas a gambler, hardly out of his novitiate, and still shying instinctively at the name, is slow to acknowledge to himself the source of his unease.

Heseltine's recognition of what ailed him was further delayed by the fact that money, the common objective of gamblers, was of no interest to him. He ceased to take in the financial papers. He had instructed Lockhart to switch his surviving holdings into British Government securities and to leave them alone. He never glanced at City news. As far as money-making went, he had done with it.

None the less, the itch for his daily dram of pleasurable excitement continued to harass him. The insipidity, the savourless routine of his life in Beaumont Street got him down. He looked back with nostalgia to the last three years; not to his dream, which had gone the way of all dreams, but to the petty, diurnal satisfactions of the throw, the suspense, the dénouement. And at last he came face to face with the truth: he was an addict of chance, and gamble he must.

But for what was he to gamble, if not for cash? It must be for something he valued; the chips must be exchangeable for something solid, concrete, which should satisfy a positive need of his own. The suspense must be resolved by the loss or gain of some palpable enjoyment.

For some days after his self-confession he sought in vain for a suitable objective. And then, on a Sunday afternoon, after a long walk over Shotover, he found himself, with a mile or more to go, hungrily looking forward to his tea and crumpets. And the idea came to him in a flash. Supposing he were to toss up, "heads I have tea, tails I go without!" To win would be a solid satisfaction, to lose a real deprivation. He had got it! In future he would gamble for his meals.

Heseltine was not a greedy man, but he enjoyed his food and looked forward to it. When he entered his cosy sitting-room, and saw the small tea-table by the fire, the crumpets on the hearth, he knew that the spin of the coin would matter to him. He took a florin from his trouser pocket, spun it, and let it fall upon the hearthrug. Heads! Never before had he relished his crumpets as he relished them that day.

But as he sat in his armchair after tea, lined with crumpets and smoking his pipe, he reflected that the spinning of a coin was a very poor technique. The suspense, lasting about one second, while he bent towards the hearthrug to discover which side of the coin was uppermost, had been nothing at all. He must improve on that. Then another thing struck him. Should he then and there, full-fed as he was, make a throw for his dinner, even by some method whereby the suspense should be more prolonged, he would be incapable of caring whether he won his meal or lost it. The toss for tea had been exciting, for an instant, because he was hungry and the dish of crumpets had been there before his eyes. He must time his future throws to coincide with the flow, not the ebb, of appetite.

Further considerations occurred to him. Should he dine in his lodgings, as was his habit three or four times a week, there would be the question of due notice to his landlady, Mrs Mullens. But Mrs Mullens, who did her shopping in the mornings, expected her orders after breakfast. Heseltine liked to eat a good breakfast, with the result that immediately after it he could take no such interest in luncheon, let alone dinner, as could conceivably lead to excitement while he threw the dice or turned the cards. Appetite and Mrs Mullens could never be present together. And what about breakfast itself? If he played for it when he woke, the excitement would be there, but on losing days he would be compelled to ring for Mrs Mullens and cancel the meal. Not only would the sausages, the bacon, the kippers, the kidneys be wasted, but Mrs Mullens, who was almost vexatiously motherly, would want to call the doctor. And yet to play for his breakfast overnight would be futile. He himself would be thrill-proof after his dinner, and Mrs Mullens, should he lose the throw and countermand the breakfast, no less fussily concerned than in the morning.

Pondering these complications, Heseltine decided that he must make a change in his accustomed routine. In future he would lunch and dine at the Gridiron, except on those nights when he dined in College. (For the College, on his resignation, had made him an honorary member of the Senior Common Room, and welcomed him to the High Table whenever he felt inclined for company.) The Grid did not serve breakfasts, but he would breakfast at the Randolph Hotel. And he would tell Mrs Mullens to adjust his rent in such a way as to recoup herself for the modest profit she made upon his meals. With such a routine, he would be free to play for each meal at such times as hunger, or at any rate appetite, should make the winning or losing of it a matter of consequence to himself.

His thoughts then reverted to the question of technique. Tossing was no good. He thought of dicing, but he knew nothing of calculating probabilities, and had no idea of the number of throws in which the chance of a double-six would be equal, for or against. In any case throwing dice was monotonous. The most satisfactory way, he concluded, would be the turning of cards. If he had two packs, one marked "Eat" and the other "Starve" he could turn the cards alternately, as slowly as he liked, and the winning pack would be that from which all four aces first appeared. Suspense could be prolonged by deliberation in turning, and as the aces began to show themselves, from this pack or that, the excitement, to a man often sharp set from the loss of the previous meal, would be the very thing he was looking for.

Having made his decision, Heseltine knocked out his pipe and sat himself at his work-table, where his notebooks on Carteret lay neatly stacked. But he could not bring his mind to his task. He felt himself to be on the eve of a holiday, and his thoughts ranged pleasurably about the bitter-sweet savour of his future existence. The clock recalled him to himself. Being Sunday night, he was due to dine in College, and it was time to dress. Having, as yet, no pack of cards, he had not proposed to play for this night's dinner; but he realised that, had he wished to gamble for it, he would have been indifferent to the result of the throw. For he was not only not hungry, he had no feeling of appetite at all. This brought home to him the recognition that, after crumpets for tea, he rarely or never did have an appetite for dinner. He ate dinner as a matter of habit, enjoying, but not needing, it. Under the new régime, assuming that, over a period, his wins and losses would be about equal, he would, in fact, halve the number of his meals and, by so doing, double the enjoyment of those left to him. This fresh aspect of the thing delighted him. The sharper the edge of his appetite, the bigger the thrill of the cards. A further satisfaction he had hitherto overlooked was that this halving of meals would about make up to him the extra expense of eating at the Grid and the Randolph. For Heseltine had an economical side to him. He went into Hall in high spirits and his colleagues decided that he must have broken the back of Carteret at last.

Next morning he ate his last breakfast cooked by Mrs Mullens, and having, with more difficulty than he had foreseen (since Mrs Mullens's pride in her cooking suffered a wound), come to terms with his landlady, he went out to buy his cards. He bought two packs, one of cards with red tartan backs, one of cards with green tartan backs. On returning to his rooms, he carefully shuffled each pack, threw out the jokers, replaced them in their cases, and marked the red case EAT and the green case STARVE. With the feeling that his future was secure, Heseltine returned to Carteret with more attention than of late, and it was past one o'clock, his usual luncheon hour, when he began to feel a mild, but by no means insistent, inclination towards food. He did not want to be disappointed with his first trial of the cards, and had almost decided to skip lunch, and make sure of a thrill over tea, when he prudently recollected that he might well lose tea, and dinner as well. In which case the loss of his luncheon would be a pity, to say the least. So he took out the two packs, and began turning the cards, turn and turn about, and piling those turned neatly on one side. His interest, from lack of hunger, being lukewarm, he did not bother to prolong the suspense by slow motion. He turned the cards briskly, and when the fourth ace from STARVE appeared against two from EAT, he was, on the whole, pleased. He knew he would be ravenous for tea. He must, however, for Mrs Mullens's sake, get his hat and go out as if to the Gridiron Club.

There was a problem about tea which only now occurred to

him. He was not prepared to sacrifice, at any rate in autumn and winter, the cosy hours by his own fireside between five o'clock and six. He could, of course, if he played the cards at half-past four and lost, ring the bell and say "no tea tonight." But it would lead to coaxing and enquiries. He decided that tea could always be served, and that "no crumpets tonight" could be explained by a heavy luncheon, an early dinner or his doctor's warnings.

One o'clock is not a good hour to begin a walk at Oxford. In term-time there is nothing to see on the river or the playing-fields, and Heseltine was fond of watching both rowing and games. So he went to the Union to read the weeklies and reviews. Later on he took his usual walk, returning to Beaumont Street about four. By this time he was really hungry and decided to make the most of his gamble for tea. He turned each card with deliberation. The first ace came from EAT. The second, after a delicious suspense, from STARVE. Then two more, in rapid succession, from EAT. Three to one on the crumpets! He could almost feel them, warm and succulent, in his mouth. But the next turned up from STARVE, and so did, damn it all, its successor. It was neck and neck after all. Slowly as he was going, he went more slowly still. There were not many cards left. He had a fleeting idea of make the next ace decide his dinner as well. But he remembered the long dull hours to be got through if he yielded to the temptation, and refrained. He turned an ace: it was from STARVE. He rang the bell for Mrs Mullens.

"No crumpets for tea tonight, please, Mrs Mullens. I—er—rather overdid my luncheon."

Hungry as he was, he felt that his plan was working out. He did not even sip his tea, but filled his cup twice and poured the contents away in the bathroom, where he drank a glass of water. The next session, his hunger told him, would bring excitement indeed.

He worked rather well at Carteret for a couple of hours, his stomach having no occasion for summoning the blood from his brain. But soon after six o'clock he could wait no longer. He got out the cards, and won his dinner comfortably, by four aces to two. By seven o'clock he was at the Grid, mildly astonishing the club-waiter by ordering four courses instead of the usual three, and exhibiting chuckling good spirits to his fellow-diners.

After a few weeks Heseltine felt that on the whole the plan was working out well. He certainly, after missing two meals or more running, had known greater excitement than had ever been his during his stock-market days. No financial gain can compare, as a stake, with eggs and bacon after a twenty-four-hour fast. There were, however, one or two drawbacks in the régime which he had overlooked. He was not feeling quite so well as of old. And he was losing weight. His theory that, owing to sharper hunger, he would devour in half the number of meals as much food as before had proved fallacious. A really empty stomach has less capacity to ingest, let alone to digest, than a moderately empty one. Prolonged fasts, such as came from missing four or five meals in succession, as had happened to him, exhausted him, and the consequent "hogging" of a famished man brought on bilious attacks. But he was not yet so out of sorts as seriously to consider sacrificing a part of his daily fun to his health. He had once considered, when genuinely exhausted after a run of bad luck, weighting the odds in favour of food, by removing one ace from EAT and making the third ace a winner in that pack. But, after his next meal, he felt that to do so would be cowardly and unsportsmanlike. It could always be done, but not yet.

And then two things happened, both unfortunate and, in conjunction, fatal. The first was that Mrs Mullens, owing to the illness of a sister, was compelled to leave Oxford for Ealing. For a fortnight at the most, she hoped, but how was her lodger to manage? A charlady could be got to clean the whole house once a week, but a "daily" was not to be had at any price.

Heseltine reassured her. He had all his meals out. He was quite capable of making his own bed and, if necessary, of lighting his own fire. But the weather was mild, and in any case he had the Union and the Senior Common Room as refuges. So Mrs Mullens went, on a Monday morning. The charlady was to come that day week.

The second misfortune happened on the same Monday morning, before lunch. Heseltine had played for his luncheon and lost. Before putting away the packs he had brushed, with his sleeve, a few cards—about half a dozen—from the top of the red tartan pack on to the floor at the side of the table. There they lay, full in view, and ready to his hand. He picked them up, replaced them on the pack, shuffled it, and put both packs into their respective cases. He then went off to the Union before taking his usual walk.

But one card, in falling from the table, had not fallen upon the carpet. It had dropped, silent as a leaf, into the waste-paper basket, where it remained, as ill-luck would have it, on edge, close against the side. And before leaving his room Heseltine had thrown into the same basket a handful of torn envelopes from his morning mail. These were enough to smother the card, which happened to be an ace.

It was the end. The EAT pack could no longer win. Heseltine was still to enjoy, with a crescendo of excitement, amounting at last to a very agony of hope and fear, a dozen more sessions. But on the Friday morning his exhaustion was so great that he decided, as he lay in bed, to breakfast at the Randolph, and, for the future, to weight the cards in favour of EAT. So light-headed was he that he could not for the life of him remember whether, in order to do this, he must draw an ace from the red or the green. He would eat first, he decided. But on getting out of bed, Heseltine fainted and fell, headlong, hitting the back of his head against the brass fender. And there, four days later, the charlady found him.

At the inquest, the medical evidence was that the deceased had undoubtedly been concussed by the fall, but the true cause of death was inanition. It was likely, the doctor thought, that he had recovered consciousness, but must have been too feeble, from starvation, to help himself. His friends and colleagues could only hope that the doctor had been wrong, and that their dear Marcus had not, alone on that bedroom floor, been conscious—who knows for how many hours or even days—of his forlorn plight. But how that tranquil and self-controlled don came to die of starvation was a mystery none of them could solve.

His Crowded Hour

It was before Hitler's war, when a word like "glory" could still be applied to certain occasions in civilian life, that I found myself sitting beside the little old man on a bench in Regent's Park. He dated himself, within a decade or so, when he asked if I could oblige him with a "lucifer." He was a thin, under-nourished old fellow and dreadfully shabby, but the long white locks that fell over his coat-collar were carefully combed, and he had a bright, self-satisfied eye. We soon fell into talk, and I noticed the care with which he enunciated, as if his speech had been acquired by study rather than native to him. But he was full of topics, and it flowed easily enough.

When the exchange of generalities had lasted long enough to create that bond between chance acquaintances which, however slender, permits of a more personal turn, he turned to face me, after a pause, and said:

"Have you, sir, I wonder now, ever enjoyed the greatest experience in the world?"

It was not the sort of enquiry one expects from a shabby stranger in the park, and I was a bit taken aback, particularly by his assumption that the greatest experience in the world was a known thing, something that both of us, should it come to us, would recognise as such. Nor could I suppress an unworthy suspicion that he wanted our talk to take an erotic turn. The greatest common experience in the world—well, love-making could make a strong case for itself there.

So I answered rather coolly:

"I can't say, without knowing what you mean by 'the greatest experience.' One man's meat can be another man's poison."

"Ah," he said, "then it's clear that you have never had it, sir. If you had, you'd have answered pat enough, I'll be bound." There was a note of triumph in his voice. I knew I should not have to ask him what it was. He was about to disclose it, with gusto. I was right.

"The greatest experience in the world, sir," he announced, leaning forward, "is applause."

The authority in his voice was absolute. There was no question but that he knew what he was talking about. This shabby waif had been applauded, and applauded to the echo. That was a certainty.

He now wore so superior an air as he waited for my comment that I should have liked to take him down a peg. To say "Oh, applause? Well yes, I admit it's pleasant enough at the time" and then, if possible, to have yawned, ever so slightly. But what did I know of applause? Some clapping from the grandstand at Henley when we won the Ladies' Plate; some champagne-begotten yells from undergraduates after a bump-supper speech: occasions that came and went and left no mark. I could no more claim, on such grounds as these, to know about applause than I could pretend to be a critic of opera because I sang in my bath. There was nothing for it but to capitulate.

"I can well imagine that," I said. "It must be wonderful."

He was pleased with my surrender.

"That's just what it is, sir," he said. "Wonderful. The greatest experience in the world. And it stays with you for ever."

"So I see," I said, rather unkindly, but his eyes by now were alight with memories, and he was past being ruffled.

"Yes, sir," he went on, "to have enjoyed such applause as has been given to myself sweetens life. It's not every man that can say, when he has come to my age, that he has lived to some purpose. It's a wonderful satisfaction."

"It must be," I said. "So you were on the stage?" I hazarded.

Neither his face, nor figure, nor the precautions he took with his accent would have suggested an actor.

"The London Hippodrome. Eighteen ninety-seven," he replied. "The greatest hit ever. It was a wow, if you will excuse the expression."

I hope my face showed that I excused it.

"His Royal Highness the Prince of Wales rolled in his seat, I've been told. Of course the papers could not say that, but I had it from an eye-witness. Rolled about in his seat. And the laughter! The habitués came night after night, and you got so that you could pick 'em out by the noises they made. There was a man used to crow like a cock, couldn't help himself, and an old gentleman who creaked up and down, up and down like a pump-handle. I can hear him now. As for the women, hysterics was nothing to it. Burst their stays often enough, I dare say. I tell you, sir, it was a thing to rejoice the heart, that laughter was, and to know that yours truly was the cause of it!"

"It must have been," I said. "I envy you indeed."

"Mind you," he went on, "I had to work for it. You don't get results like those without pain and grief. There were times my back and legs ached so I thought I should never go through with it. But our stage-doorman used to rub 'em with oil. Good-natured little chap he was, and a rare hand at rubbing. I was getting two pound ten a week, but he never would take a penny. 'It's for the cause, Joe,' he used to say. The great cause, sir, of making the public happy, that's what he was referring to."

"So you were a dancer?" I asked.

"You could hardly call it dancing," he said. "It was a peculiar art, mine was. You could have called me a specialist, I suppose. But the strain was mostly on the legs. Back-ache, too, I suffered from. Not to mention the heat. But so long as it made them happy—and happy they were, I can tell you."

"It must certainly be a wonderful experience," I said, "to look down upon a sea of eager, laughing faces."

He cut me short.

"That was one I did *not* have, sir. Circumstances were against it. But the noise was enough for me—the clapping, the shouting, the roaring, you might say. Every night for three mortal months."

"What was the name of the show?" I asked.

"It was Pantomime, sir. *Puss in Boots*. But the turn that brought the house down was Moko the Marvellous Donkey. Ran a full fifteen minutes, it did, not to speak of encores. And it was my honour and privilege to play the Donkey's hind-legs."

"You must let me shake your hand," I said, offering my own. "All my life I have wanted to meet the actor who did that."

"You mean you saw Moko?" he asked.

"On my way to go to school for the first time," I said. "I didn't know laughing could hurt so much, or that bellies have such a sense of humour."

He beamed. It was then I made a false step.

"And who played the fore-legs?" I asked.

"Chap called Montgomery," he said coldly. "But there's nothing in doing the fore-legs. You can see, for one thing, through the Donkey's mouth. And you're all but upright. Only got to lift your knees and stamp. Child's play, it is."

"I suppose so," I said.

He turned a severe eye upon me.

"You just try kicking both legs at once when you're bent double in the dark and can hardly breathe for the fug," he said. "You just try it, sir. You'll not want to talk about fore-legs again after that."

I assured him that I should never want to talk about fore-legs again, and he was appeased.

"I'll tell you a disgraceful thing, sir, if you'll not repeat it. That Montgomery got three pounds a week. But I don't want it known. It might upset my friends. And after all, the Art's the thing, not the money."

If ever a capital A was expressed by intonation, it was in his way of saying "Art."

"How right you are," I said. "And how long was your career on the stage?"

"Three months," he said. "Just those three months at the Hippodrome in '97. To tell the truth, I hadn't the back for the job. It let me down, my back did. So I went in for newspapers."

"Journalism?"

"No, sir, selling them. The steadiest trade there is. It's not riches, but it's regular. And just look what I have to look back on."

"You have indeed," I said, getting up. "The greatest experience in the world."

"Sir," he said, "you've taken the very words out of my mouth."

He beamed again, and we shook hands, and I said how proud I was to be doing it. And with that I turned away, but he called me back.

"I'm ashamed to trouble you again, sir," he said. "But could you possibly oblige me with another lucifer?"

Moderately Good Fellows

PATTERNE BREWSTER, known to his friends as Pincher, was as selfish as they come. But being immensely rich and naturally jovial, he passed for a good fellow. And although his ruling principle was to exchange fun for fun, mostly in the form of sport, with other rich men, he had a few old cronies, dating from his school-days, from whom he asked nothing in return but their company and their skill with gun or rod. Two of these were Tom Brown, a retired Cavalry Colonel, and Jack Robinson, a hard-working Q.C. The three had been boys together; they shared, together with old jokes, a hundred memories of shooting, fishing and stalking days, and Tom and Jack always maintained, against the world, that, so long as you took care not to know him, Pincher was quite a good chap. They themselves, for the sake of an annual fortnight at Brewster's lodge in the Forest of Glen Damph, and a week's partridge-driving at Hare Park, had, by dint of determination and circumspection, succeeded in restricting their knowledge of their old pal to the most superficial level. They had trained themselves to see in him what they wanted to see—an agreeable and merry provider of excellent sport—and no more.

The Forest of Glen Damph, in the heart of Ross-shire, has everything a keen stalker could desire. It comprises a group of long-backed mountains, high but not precipitous, linked to one another by accommodating saddles, and buttressed with spurs that flank a series of corries, deep or shallow, narrow or wide. The feeding is good; there is shelter, let the wind blow from whatever quarter, and the deer, reassured by ample sanctuary in which no man ever sets foot, grow heavy bodies and, not infrequently, royal heads. Along the western march flows the Black Burn full of brown trout, into a loch overlooked by the Lodge. For those who know the Highlands, the beauty of this kind of country need not be described; to those who do not, a description could only give rise to heartache. To Pincher himself, whose lot had fallen in so fair a ground, the landscape meant little. He enjoyed a fine day, but the forest was to him the home of the red deer. To his two old cronies, on the other hand, the great hills themselves, the incessant and subtle changes of colour, the mysterious recessions of the corries, a mountain's intimacies and withdrawals, contributed the greater part of their delight. Keen stalkers as they were, it could be said that eighty per cent of their enjoyment came from the magnificence of their surroundings. And subconsciously, no doubt, the feeling that so much of their pleasure derived from a source for which their host had no responsibility, did something to mitigate that secret uneasiness with which most of us accept benefits at the hands of a man we like but cannot respect, benefits for which we can make no return in kind.

The forest was divided, for stalking purposes, into five beats. Of these three were reserved for Pincher himself, the other two for his guests. At the time of my story, Pincher's attitude to stalking had reached a climax to which he had long and gradually been approaching. With advancing years, the physical exhilaration of a day on the hills meant less and less to him; he had come to the point of stalking mainly, if not entirely, for the sake of obtaining an outstandingly good "head." On several occasions in the past he, or one of his guests, had brought in a head which had ranked as the "best of the year"; photographs and measurements had appeared in the *Field* or *Country Life*; his forest was being talked about. The credit, of course, was due to his head-stalker, Donald Menzies, who, in Pincher's prentice years, had insisted that vigorous young stags with royal heads should be spared, and host and guests alike encouraged to feel that to rid the forest of a switch, a hummel, or any heavy beast whose antlers were on the down-grade, was their proper objective.

But now that this policy had borne good fruit, Pincher felt that the time had come to make the most of it. There were royal heads on the ground enough and to spare; and there were rich men, even socially distinguished men, with forests of their own, who would not despise a day at Glen Damph. Pincher's social ambitions had increased with the years; and there came a day when he asked himself why he should any longer restrict the purchasing-power of his celebrated forest by wasting precious days and beats on a retired Colonel of cavalry and a barrister, neither of whom had either fun or prestige to offer in return?

Pincher was not a man who, having seen where his advantage lies, is slow to act. He decided to drop Brown and Robinson. But how? He greatly cherished his reputation as a good fellow. He disliked the idea of his friends, who were much fonder of Tom and Jack than they were of himself, asking one another if they had heard the latest about Pincher: that he had rubbed out those two nice chaps to make room for a Duke and a Cabinet Minister? He was still more afraid of what Donald Menzies would think. Donald Menzies, a tall, handsome, blue-eyed Scot of great truth and simplicity, had an ascendancy over his employer which Pincher secretly resented but was unable, with his own mediocre moral equipment, to resist. Menzies had not only made a stalker of Pincher: he had even, up to a point, made a good host of him. He had been unable, it is true, to persuade his master to make a fairer division of the beats as between himself and his guests, but the bald terms of his refusal, in the early days of Pincher's reign, to "give this young gentleman a good walk but don't let him get a stag," had frightened his employer into conventional good manners. Menzies was greatly attached to both Brown and Robinson, as much for themselves as for their skill and enthusiasm, and a confession to his head-stalker, of the steady blue eyes, that he had failed to invite his favourites, was a thing Pincher was determined, if possible, to evade.

It was, then, clear to him that his old pals could not be dropped like hot potatoes. But he thought that, with patience and planning, they might be edged out. For Brewster, with all his egoism, was not obtuse. He was perfectly aware of the lack of true regard felt for him by those two, as indeed by all his friends. He knew, what Tom and Jack so uncomfortably felt but tried to suppress, that their friendship for him was founded on what he had to offer, not on any qualities in himself. If he could succeed in quietly diminishing the value of his favours, were they not likely to abandon him of their own accord?

After much cogitation he formed a plan. It was not one to which either Menzies or James McKenzie, the stalker in charge of the guest-beats, could be made privy. But fortunately he had at hand a confederate on whom he felt he could rely.

A year or two earlier a man named Murdoch, head-stalker to an acquaintance of Brewster's in a distant part of Scotland, had been sacked by his employer for dishonesty. His employer was a merciful man. At the moment of his discovery of Murdoch's goings on, Brewster happened to be his guest. He took him into his confidence and, knowing how high a value Brewster put upon his own good nature, asked him if he was prepared to give the man a second chance. There was something in Brewster's make-up, of which he himself was probably not fully aware, that relished the idea of possessing a servant who would be incapable of looking at him with the candid, unflinching gaze of a Menzies or a McKenzie. He also happened to need a capable man to look after a small saw-mill on his estate. With a most winning exhibition of his famous good nature, Brewster agreed.

"Nobody here," he told Murdoch on his arrival in Glen Damph, "knows the reason of your coming. And so long as you do just what I tell you, nobody ever will know."

Murdoch, alive to the implied threat, promised obedience. It was to Murdoch, then, that Pincher turned for assistance in his scheme.

The saw-mill, and Murdoch's cottage, lay on the extreme

western march of the forest, where a cut from the Black Burn supplied the water-power for a circular saw. Immediately to the east of it rose the group of hills, Ben Croisich, Ben Dearg and Ben Clach, which formed the two guest-beats.

On the eve of the arrival of Brown and Robinson, Murdoch was sent for and briefed by Pincher. To say that Murdoch was surprised would be an understatement. But he knew himself to be in his master's hands. All he said was:

"But supposing the wund should shuft to the east?"

"Not very likely this time of year," said Pincher. "But if it does, you must get up earlier, that's all."

The rule for the guests was that they stalked on alternate days, amusing themselves on their off-days by fishing for brown trout in the Black Burn or the loch. Brown won the toss and took the first day. The weather was set fair; and as he started up the hill with James McKenzie, a fox-terrier of a man with a nose like a snipe, both were in high spirits. There was a slight, but steady, breeze from the west, and they began their climb from the foot of Ben Clach, the easternmost mountain of the group.

They soon spied deer lying among the white stones in Larig na Veachig, with more than one shootable stag among them. The larig itself lay high, and to get above their beasts the stalkers had a long, steep trudge, out of sight of their quarry, almost to the top of the hill. In an hour and a half of hard going they reached the ridge and, after a short breather, went cautiously forward for another look at the deer. To their consternation the deer were now standing up. Only a couple of hinds, something downhill from the rest, were grazing. The others were alert and restless. In no time they had decided to move, and move they did, falling into single file behind a heavy stag with a good head, and winding down the larig till they disappeared round a shoulder. Something had disturbed them.

There was nothing for it but to start all over again. They had time in hand and the incident was all in the day's work. But although McKenzie soon spied more beasts in approachable spots, and attempted four promising stalks, they all came to nothing, and Brown never got a shot. The deer would never settle; they were uneasy and restless, never taking positive fright, but ever on the move. The vexed and taciturn McKenzie decided that he had never known such a thing.

The second day was much like the first. Robinson and McKenzie, starting this time from the eastern foot of Ben Dearg, spied beasts enough, but could never come up with them. At the proper hours for chewing the cud the deer were travelling instead. On one occasion, when Robinson was actually crawling in for a shot with a steady wind in his face, the stag with his smaller companions, sprang to his feet, and all their noses went up together. They went off at a canter.

"They've wunded a man," said McKenzie. "I'm wondering could it be the new minister at Achnacarrish. He's awfu' set on access to mountains and such foolishness."

But the minister, when he did break loose, used to walk the ridges in a black coat, and invariably came into view sooner or later. There was no sign of him that day.

And so it went on. There was the day when the forest seemed almost bare of beasts and McKenzie, taking a spy from Ben Croisich into the sanctuary to the north, found the deer "just cumbering the ground" on the slopes of that forbidden enclave.

"You would think they had been driven like sheep," he remarked.

Donald Menzies, at the end of each day, when relaying McKenzie's puzzled reports to his employer, used to fix Pincher with a glance too piercing for that good fellow to meet. But if he dropped his eyes, he was chuckling to himself, and when the seventh successive blank day was reported, he could see in his mind's eye the welcome letters of embarrassed refusal which he would receive, next June, from Robinson and Brown in reply to his routine invitations to stalk. For Pincher judged others by himself.

In truth, of course, his treachery was getting him nowhere. Brown and Robinson, in that wonderful weather, on those incomparable high tops, had been enjoying themselves hugely. To them, as has been said, the kill was but a minor element in their enjoyment. They were sorry for McKenzie's chagrin, but were fascinated by the spectacle of deer so alert, and amused and interested by the stalker's exasperated speculations as to the cause of it. Not once did it occur to them that they had any grievance, even against luck.

So that, but for an accident, Pincher's plan would have altogether miscarried. Owing to the accident, it succeeded, but at a price.

The accident was to Murdoch's right ankle. On the eighth day the wind suddenly went round to the east, and Murdoch had to get up very early indeed, and make some lengthy detours, and climb several high ridges, before he returned at night to his cottage on the western march. The result was that darkness overtook him descending the last hill and he turned an ankle in the loose stones.

It was ten o'clock that evening before Murdoch's boy arrived at the Lodge with a note for his master. Pincher was not in his usual spirits that evening, for Robinson had shot a beast at last, a nice ten-pointer, the east wind having set Murdoch a problem that even that crafty hillsman could not quite solve. Excusing himself to his guests, Pincher rang up Menzies and told him that he had changed his mind, and wouldn't be stalking on the morrow.

During the night the wind again went round to the west. Having no engagement with his employer, Menzies decided to accompany the Colonel and McKenzie. Early as they started, they heard that Pincher had left the lodge earlier still, in the small car he used for the mountain roads.

When the head-stalker was present, McKenzie acted as ghillie, but Menzies, with his highland good manners, took care to consult with his lieutenant on every move. They began again at the foot of Ben Clach, and soon spied beasts. But once again, on coming up to their quarry, they found the deer on the move. A fresh stalk was begun, and a long one, but in the middle of it they were astonished at the sight of a bunch of deer coming over a ridge towards them at the gallop.

"It was no a taste of the wund that set that lot going," said Menzies. "It wull be something they seen that affrighted them, puir beasts."

It was useless to continue with their stalk, and they decided to lunch and to give what deer might be in front of them a chance to settle. During lunch the two stalkers, sitting as always apart from the rifle, talked together in Gaelic. After a more leisurely lunch than is usual, Menzies came across to Brown.

"If the Colonel will excuse me," he said, "I will be away on my own, just to take a look-see. It's no natural, what's going on hereabouts. If the Colonel will wait half an hour, McKenzie will try for a beast south on Ben Dearg, but I'm no very hopefu'."

Donald Menzies strode away, at a speed that slackened only on the steepest slopes, and making first towards the northern march, he later swung westward, and making good with his spy-glass every fresh slope and corrie as it came into sight, he finally rounded the top of Ben Croisich and looked down upon the Black Burn. Along its further bank snaked a rough road, of which, from his vantage point, Menzies could see about a mile, running south from the saw-mill and McGregor's farmhouse to the loch and the lodge. Menzies first of all turned his spy-glass upon the saw-mill. It was working, and he had a glimpse of Murdoch limping across from the saw-pit. About half a mile below the saw-mill a wooden footbridge gave access from the road to the Forest of Glen Damph. It was upon this point that the head-stalker next turned his telescope, and as he had more than half-expected, he spotted a small car parked in a primitive lay-by close to the footbridge. Cautiously creeping, with many a pause for spying, beneath the ridge of Ben Croisich, and parallel with the Burn, he finally spied what he now wholly expected—the figure of his employer cautiously, and for an amateur creditably, dodging his way down the mountain towards the footbridge. Menzies closed his telescope with a snap, crawled back over the ridge, and made his way home.

The head-stalker, made aware by occasional conversations with Murdoch that the new sawyer had a thorough knowledge of deer and their ways, had been growing, for several days past, increasingly suspicious. But the sight of the galloping deer that morning, coupled with his employer's change of plan and early start from the lodge, had caused him to switch his suspicions from man to master. Only an amateur would have blundered on deer in such a way as to startle them into a panic. And Murdoch's talk had been that of a professional.

But it is possible strongly to suspect, and yet to be shocked at discovering that one's suspicions are justified. Menzies was not only shocked, but embarrassed. As a Highlander, he knew hospitality to be a sacred thing. As a servant, he was accustomed to discourage in himself critical thoughts of his employer. As Donald Menzies, he had much regard and affection for the Colonel and Musterr Robunson. By the time he reached home, he had made up his mind that the breach of hospitality, and the obligation of friendship, must be first attended to. As chance had it, the Colonel returned from a fruitless afternoon on Ben Dearg a few minutes later. Menzies was at his cottage door as the Colonel passed and, as often before, stopped him to enquire "What luck?" But this time he asked the Colonel very gravely to step inside. And there he told him of his discovery.

The Colonel at first found difficulty in believing it. If Pincher was tired of his old friends, why all this elaborate sport-spoiling? He had only to leave them out of next year's invitations. Besides, he hadn't spoilt their fun: it had all been most enjoyable. But there is no arguing with a Highlander about what has happened on his own hills. In the end he was forced to accept the fact that Pincher had not been playing cricket.

"I don't think Mr Robinson and I can stay on here," he said. "Of course we shall give nothing away. We can easily invent some excuse."

Menzies fixed him with an innocent blue eye. "It seems a putty that the Colonel and Musterr Robunson should cut shorrt their holiday," he said. "Mrs McGregor at yon farrm beyont the Black Burrn has verra decent rooms for gentlemen who come for the fushin'. An' she's a good cook. If the Colonel and Musterr Robunson were to shuft their things to McGregor's, they could maybe have some good days with the trout."

"But suppose this fine weather holds, Menzies? The burn's pretty low, and it's not much good fishing in this sunshine."

"That is so," said Menzies, "but the gentlemen might care to take a walk on the hill instead."

"But that's all Heskernich ground beyond the march, isn't it? We can't go tramping about another man's forest."

"God forbid!" said Menzies. "But I was thunking, I could let ye know each night the beat where Mr Brewster will be stalking the morn, and the gentlemen, being his friends, might see no harm in taking a walk in that direction."

"You old devil," said the Colonel. "I didn't know you had it in you. It's a brain-wave. I love walking. So does Mr Robinson. How soon could you see about those rooms?"

"I'll have Angus away on his machine this verra minute," said Menzies. And he did.

Brown went into the Lodge and had a talk to Robinson. At dinner that evening they were silent and depressed, and over the port the Colonel spoke up.

"Pincher, old boy, you won't be hurt, will you, if Jack and I wind up our holidays with a few days' fishing at Mrs McGregor's? You've given us every chance, and it has been great fun in its way, but when luck is out, it is out. Fact is, we're not as young as we were, and the hills get higher every year. And when one can't get a shot, they seem higher still. We need a rest. So if you don't mind, we'll be off in the morning."

Pincher's heart leapt within him. His plan had worked. But he remembered what a good fellow he was.

"Of course I'm not hurt. How could you think such a thing? But you must stop on and do your fishing from here."

"Good of you," said Brown, "but we couldn't think of it. You'll need our rooms—you can't leave all that grand ground alone at the peak of the season. The stags will be roaring any time now."

Pincher's heart again smiled within him. "There's something in that, of course. My nephews will come on a wire—I'd been feeling a little guilty about them this year."

And on the following morning Brown and Robinson, having agreed about tips, went off in one of Pincher's cars to Mrs McGregor's farmhouse.

They had little luck with the trout that day, but in the evening Angus arrived on his bicycle with a note. "Ben More" was all that was written on it.

It was a five-mile walk down the burn to the western foothills of Ben More, but the west wind still held. Although it was some years since either had stalked on the Ben More beat, in the old days, when Pincher himself was a learner and had not yet reserved three-fifths of the forest to his own use, they had both been over it often enough. Slow as they were, like all amateurs, at spying, and fearful of blundering into sight of beasts, they had a pretty good idea of what contours to follow in order to taint, by their presence, the breezes which would blow over this or that face, flow and eddy into this or that corrie, of the many-folded slopes and shoulders which buttressed, on the east, the massive ridge of Ben More. In an appreciable breeze, deer will detect the presence of a man at a mile or more. There are corries, of course, where the wind will "whurrl" to a point where a west wind will reach the nose of a stag as from the east. To a stalking-party, coming up-wind, this can be fatal. But to Brown and Robinson it mattered not at all. Let the deer move in what direction they would, provided that they moved.

The fact that there were two of them to Murdoch's one did much to compensate for their individual lack of speed, and Menzies, stalking from the east with Pincher, was highly satisfied with his gentlemen's performance. Beasts were on the move all day and Pincher never got a shot.

Being rich enough to have saddle-ponies waiting for him at

all likely points of departure to, and return from, the hill, Pincher had contrived so to mitigate the exertion of a day's stalking that he rarely took a day off. Accordingly, Brown and Robinson were not surprised when Angus again appeared at dinner-time with a note which read: "Very good. The Spoots."

It would be tedious to recount the doings of the ensuing days. It need only be said that Brown and Robinson, defeated on one occasion, as even Murdoch had been defeated, by an easterly wind, succeeded in spoiling five days out of six for that good fellow, their host. After which, they returned to London and their clubs.

They saw no reason to hold their tongues about Pincher's treachery. It made a good story, and they told it. And in no time, of course, it got round to Pincher.

His cherished reputation for being a jolly good fellow, always somewhat precariously balanced, was now dished indeed. People were even rude enough openly to chaff him about it.

"Hullo, Pincher. I hear your stags have got such delicate noses that they can no longer be approached," and so on.

What was he to do? What would a good chap do? To invite the Cabinet Minister and the Scottish Duke, as he had promised to himself, would be fatal. After much unhappy cogitation, he decided that he had one slender chance of living down his folly. When May came round, he wrote as usual to Brown and Robinson to ask them for a fortnight's stalking in September.

The two friends, who received their letters by the same post, agreed on the telephone to lunch together at Brooks's.

"What cheek!" said Robinson.

"A hide like a rhinoceros," said Brown.

"About that, I'm not so sure," said Robinson. "They tell me the old boy's been dreadfully down in the mouth."

"I should hope so," said Brown.

"Where are you going this summer?" asked Robinson.

"God knows," said Brown. "Wherever it is, I shall be thinking of Glen Damph. Twenty years is a long time."

"The happiest days of my life," said Robinson. "Who'd have thought he could have played us such a trick?"

"I don't know about that," said Brown. "We've always known that he was selfish as be damned."

"More fools us for playing with him," said Robinson.

"We've had a lot of fun out of it, all the same," said Brown. "Pincher has a lot of charm when he likes."

"He certainly has," said Robinson. "Look at that letter," and he tossed his invitation across the table to Brown.

"I nearly cried when I got mine this morning," said Brown.

"He's certainly had his punishment," said Robinson.

"Which is supposed to expiate the crime," said Brown.

"Even a dog is given a second chance," said Robinson.

"What about giving old Pincher one?" said Brown.

"To forgive would be a Christian act," said Robinson.

"Seventy times seven," quoted Brown.

And so it was settled. They wrote charming notes of acceptance to Pincher, and September found the three old friends once again at Glen Damph.

Not that things were quite the same as before. Donald Menzies, as a Highlander, never forgave; and his manner towards his old friends Brown and Robinson carried a hint of disapproval. Nor could those candid blue eyes of his meet, with their pristine fearlessness, those of the master he had betrayed. The eternal hills alone remained unchanged, as bountiful as before to the four men who roamed them, and knew themselves, and each other, to be but moderately good fellows.

Father Lascaut bears False Witness

ALTHOUGH Father Lascaut, the junior of the two secretaries of the Bishop of Tremblans, had been for many years the most loyal and devoted of servants, there came a day when it seemed to Bishop and secretary alike that a change might be good for both of them. The Bishop, humble as he was, felt an increasing desire to have, on occasions, his own way instead of his secretary's way, be it never so efficient; and the secretary, on his side, found himself more and more often looking back with longing to the days when he had been his own master, and could do the obviously right thing without subterfuge, and without having to explain, even when weary, why its rightness was obvious. So when a vacancy occurred for a Curé at Arcaubon, a large parish at the far end of the diocese, it struck both men simultaneously that this might be the answer to their unexpressed wishes.

But it is one thing to share a thought; quite another to make a mutual discovery of it. For a day or two after the announcement of the death of the venerable Curé of Arcaubon, they limited their comments on the occasion to praise of the good old man. But his place must be filled, and it was Father Lascaut who made the first move.

"I wonder, Excellency, what you would have said had it been I who had died as Curé of Arcaubon?"

"You, my son?" said the Bishop. "I should have been deeply grieved, and I hope I should have said that it was a dreadful loss to the parish."

"You hope, but you are not sure, Excellency?"

"My memory is still good," said the Bishop.

"And mine," said the priest. "But there's a saying: 'third time lucky.' It has always been my ambition to be a dreadful loss to some parish when I die."

"And you would like the people of Arcaubon to be the ones to lament you?"

"As well as any others. All men are born to sorrow."

"I will think it over," said the Bishop. Actually, he had been thinking it over since the moment he knew of the vacancy, so in no time the thing was settled.

Father Lascaut was happy at Arcaubon. He had learnt much during his years with the Bishop, especially how to get his own way while allowing others to believe it was theirs. But the Bishop was not so fortunate. In a matter of weeks he was bitterly regretting that he had parted with his junior secretary. for his senior secretary, Father Menegal, who, with Father Lascaut at his elbow, had served his chief, if not with brilliance, satisfactorily enough, was now proving himself to be a broken reed. Steadfast in devotion as he was, he was a muddler, slow, obtuse, and incapable of decision.

The Bishop decided that Father Menegal must go. It was hard to discharge so faithful and well-meaning a servant, but the business of the Diocese was suffering, and the Bishop felt that he had no choice in the matter. So he took the bull by the horns and, having decided that the best time for a painful interview is ten o'clock on a sunny morning, he sent for Father Menegal at that hour on the first fine day and broke the poor man's heart.

What made it worse for Menegal was that he had no inkling of his own shortcomings. He knew himself to be conscientious and hard-working; his affection for his Bishop was dog-like and unquestioning; to himself, his slow and muddled ways were the methods of a cautious man who could see all sides of a problem. So the shock of his dismissal was shattering.

In his distress, one might say his despair, his thoughts turned at once to Father Lascaut. If any man had influence with the Bishop it was Lascaut. And who, better than Lascaut, knew the merits of his former colleague? He sat down at once and wrote, in his misery, a pathetic and moving letter, beseeching his kind friend to intercede on his behalf.

Father Lascaut, who had a real affection for the man whose faults he had for so many years shielded and concealed, was much moved by Father Menegal's appeal. He sat down at once and wrote a letter to the Bishop, setting down at some length all the virtues possessed by his late colleague. He praised his conscience, his industry, his faithfulness, his integrity, his self-lessness, his devotion, and so on and so on. He ended by begging the Bishop to have second thoughts.

Father Lascaut had long ago made one very good rule for himself: never to post an important letter until he had slept over it. Accordingly, he slept over this one.

Next morning, while shaving, he thought over his letter. And he saw, in a flash, that it would never do. Everything he had said about Menegal was already known to the Bishop. The Bishop's intimacy with Menegal had been longer, by several years, than his own. The Bishop was a just and generous man. Before deciding to part with Menegal he must have weighed all his virtues to a scruple. There could be no point whatever, no possible advantage for his unhappy friend, in reminding the Bishop of things he knew only too well.

Father Lascaut went downstairs and tore up the letter, wondering how he could have been so obtuse as to waste time in writing it. He then picked up the tray which held his morning coffee and roll, and carried it into the garden. Under an umbrella-pine stood a green and ancient, though still solid, wooden table, strewn with pine-needles. Having brushed these away and brought up an iron chair, designed, he sometimes thought, to mortify the flesh of his predecessors, he sat himself down to drink his coffee, munch his roll, and consider the problem of how to help Father Menegal. To do nothing in the face of the wretched man's appeal was impossible; but what to do that could conceivably help him?

It was a hot, buzzing morning; wasps were quickly drawn to the dab of plum jam which lay in a saucer on his tray, and the hated houseflies were already busy about his head. There must also have been something that attracted them in the surface of the black japanned tray on which stood his meagre breakfast things, for they soon began to settle and crawl to and fro upon it, with a purposeful, investigatory air. The little priest was too intent upon his thoughts even to wave them away, when an unexpected apparition on the edge of the tray recalled him to actualities. It was a spider, as big as his thumbnail, standing high on strong, hairy legs, with a back covered with short grey fur, but marked, in the centre, with a black pattern which closely resembled a death's head. There was no thread by which it might have descended from the branches overhead; no web at hand from which it might have crawled. It just appeared, motionless, watchful and sinister on the bevelled edge of the tray. Father Lascaut had been long enough in Provence and regarded himself as enough of a naturalist, to be faintly annoyed at his failure to recognise and name the creature, but the feeling quickly gave way to one of astonishment when the spider made a sudden leap of at least five inches in the air to land upon the back of one of the flies. A jumping spider was new to him.

The spider remained where it had alighted, slowly manipulating its struggling victim in its jaws, with a view to sucking it dry, But Father Lascaut wanted to see the spider jump again, and managed, with a couple of pine needles, to disengage the prey from the preyer. The fly buzzed off, none the worse, but the spider remained on the spot, surprised, no doubt, but unperturbed. It even allowed Father Lascaut to replace it, with the blade of his butter-knife, upon the edge of the tray.

The flies, who had risen together when the spider jumped, immediately returned to their investigations, taking no notice of their secular enemy poised within a few inches of them. Again the spider leapt through the air; another victim was seized and rescued by the Curé; once again the imperturbable spider allowed himself to be planted on the edge of the tray, And so the game went on. By the time he was tired of it, Father Lascaut became aware, with some amusement, that he was now all on the side of the beastly flies, and against their enemy. Flies which, had he been given a quicker hand and eyes, he would have gladly swatted, he was now protecting with a warning wave of the hand, from a professional swatter who rarely missed. Why, he asked himself, this change of sympathy? The flies themselves had done nothing to alter their nature—they were the same unlovable pests as before. It was the sudden, lethal onslaught upon them by the hairy, skull-and-crossbones pirate of a spider that had swung him to championing its victims. It was then that Father Lascaut saw, in his second flash of clear-sightedness that morning, what he must do about Menegal. He must, by playing the spider, swing the Bishop's sympathies over to that poor fly Menegal. He must make an onslaught upon his old friend, so unexpected and cruel as to arouse in the Bishop the same protective instincts that the spider had awoken in himself. He got up from his chair and took a few turns along the rough garden paths, between the cistus, the tall white heaths, the myrtles, the arbutus, and the butcher-berry. A warm aroma arose from the shrubs, as unlike as could be to the harsh sentences he was arranging in his head. He then carried the breakfast-tray indoors, and sat down at his desk, in his small, cool study, to write to the Bishop. Father Lascaut was not the man, when a friend was in need, to consider the consequences to himself. Had he been such, he might have hesitated before writing the following letter:

Your Excellency,

I have received, with much concern but no surprise, a letter from Father Menegal, telling me of his dismissal. He begs me to intercede with your Excellency on his behalf, a request which, from so old a friend, I cannot refuse. It is true that there is little, if anything, that I can say about Father Menegal that your Excellency does not already know. But after seven years of daily, almost hourly, collaboration with him, it may be that I can put before your Excellency certain considerations that might enable you to take a more lenient view.

As regards his stupidity, there is of course nothing to be done; he was born like that. But might you not be worse off with a more intelligent servant? There is such a thing as being too clever by half. Besides, the bulk of mankind being stupid, it is often a convenience to have somebody on hand whose reactions will be a guide to the public's. As regards his dishonesty (of which I doubt if you are even aware) it has always been disarmingly "petty." The few odd postage-stamps, the forgotten francs in a drawer, a teaspoon dropped by the maid, a visitor's fountain-pen left on the desk—mere jackdaw pilferings. Had he ever stolen seriously I feel sure I should have discovered it; nor do I think the poor man has either the wits or the courage for a worth-while adventure into crime. It is the same with his untruthfulness—a question of mere fibs and taradiddles, as artless and transparent as a child's. As nobody could be taken in by them, they amount in fact to nothing.

On the score of loyalty, I do not think your Excellency need disturb yourself. Some men are born grumblers, and must take it out, when in bad humour, upon their superiors; but our friend knows perfectly well upon which side his bread is buttered, and a sharp word in season never fails to bring him to heel. And in any case his obtuseness is a guarantee that his little intrigues must always come to nothing.

If industry is not his strong point, I think it must be largely due to a lazy nature, which, with a weak will, he finds difficult to conquer; but here again I have found that a firm hand can do much. If I may be permitted to give your Excellency a hint, a good deal of his lethargy is undoubtedly caused by over-eating. He is invariably brisker when kept on short commons.

I hardly like to touch upon a graver matter, but in case rumours about girls have reached your Excellency, I would beg you to believe nothing that cannot be proved. Safety from scandal lies in maintaining the tradition of the Palace only to employ servants of a certain age. With old Marthe and Emilie you will have nothing to fear.

To sum up, your Excellency, I feel sure that if you could procure a watchful and intelligent colleague for our poor Menegal, you could afford to retain in your service one for whom, it has to be admitted, it will be hard indeed to find alternative employment. It may be that the priesthood was the wrong vocation for him, but he is in it for better or worse, and the lamer the dog, the greater the responsibility for turning him out of doors.

I must trust that your Excellency will forgive me for making this plea on behalf of an old friend and companion for whom, with all his shortcomings, I can wish nothing but good. Your obedient and devoted,

Lascaut.

The envelope was marked "Private and Confidential" and Menegal, through whose hands it passed, and who saw the well-known handwriting, spent a tremulous hour at his desk, examining with an unseeing eye the papers before him, rumbling internally from sheer anxiety, rising from time to time to look out of the window, as if an empty courtyard could hold a sign for a distracted man, and returning to his chair to assure himself for the hundredth time that an appeal from Lascaut would not be, could not be, must not be in vain. At the end of an hour the bell rang summoning him to the Bishop's private study. He wiped his face, he wiped the palms of his hands, and he went to hear his fate.

The Bishop looked curiously unlike himself. He was pale, and his hand, resting on the table before him, was trembling. He had the appearance of a man who had received bad news, or a shock of some sort, as indeed he had. Menegal could see Lascaut's letter on the table, but the Bishop made no reference to it.

He smiled a little wanly at his secretary, whose own white, perspiring face betrayed his misery.

"I have changed my mind, my son," said the Bishop. "You are going to remain my senior secretary. I would like you to forget some things I said to you the other day. I realise now that, without a colleague, you have been these last months under an unfair strain. I intend to remedy that. But I cannot do without you, my old friend, without your loyalty, your integrity, and your devotion. That is all."

Menegal, who wanted to cry, could only mumble his thanks, but his white face turned pink with happiness. As he walked back, on air, to his room, he felt an overwhelming sense of gratitude to his dear, generous, clever Lascaut, his rescuer and saviour. He sat down and wrote a letter of thanks that pierced its recipient's heart like a dagger. As for the Bishop, his shaken aspect had been due to the state of fury, astonishment and indignation into which Lascaut's letter had thrown him. He could hardly believe his eyes as he read such meanness, such treachery, such falsity. Lascaut, of all people!

Father Lascaut had been right. The spider's brutal onslaught had aroused an instantaneous reaction in favour of the fly, sharp enough to cause the Bishop, in his wrath, to commit himself, without further consideration, to the protection of that slandered insect. The coup had come off.

For twenty-four hours the Bishop raged within himself, reading and re-reading Lascaut's letter and wondering how to punish and bring to disgrace a man in whom for years he had been utterly deceived. And then, in the watches of the night, he suddenly saw it all. It was not a new and devilish Lascaut, it was the old impish Lascaut, wholly unscrupulous in well-doing, to whom the end was all, the means indifferent, and himself of no concern at all. With a great sigh of relief, the Bishop turned on his pillow and slept.

Next day he sent a short letter to the Curé of Arcaubon. It was as follows:

Dear Father Lascaut,

Thank you for your letter. It has succeeded in its object. For my mind, as well you know, is a slow one, and it is indeed fortunate for our friend Menegal that I was not able to see you wink as you wrote it.

Your father in God

✠ L. Tremblans.

With that letter in his pocket, Father Lascaut felt himself absolved from any need to mention, at his next confession, that he had committed the atrocious sin of bearing false witness against his neighbour.

The Six Bars Copper Mine

SIR JOCELYN BURNHAM, formerly of the Foreign Office, had
been dining at the Travellers' with his old friend Ikey Brown,
and afterwards, like the pair of comfort-loving old buffers that
they were, they sat with their brandy and cigars on the leather
sofa at the end of the big room downstairs.

Brown, known to all his friends as Ikey ever since he joined
the City firm of Cohen Brothers (later Cohen, Brown and
Company), had lately retired from business, in which he had
made a very tidy fortune. Like most Civil Servants who, however successful in their official careers, have to end their days
on somewhat slender pensions, Burnham had a good deal of
curiosity about the City. He regarded himself as no less able,
and quite as hard-working as Brown. Both had started from
scratch, and here was Brown with two grandsons at Eton while
Burnham's were at a Grammar School. Had Brown, he wondered, been particularly lucky, or might he, too, had he chosen
the City instead of the Foreign Office, have ended his days in
affluence? He was not exactly envious, for he had had a good
life. But he wanted to know how Brown had done it.

Brown was willing enough to talk about his career, and of
various big deals in which his firm had been concerned, but, so
far as Burnham could see, there seemed to have been no element of luck in any of them. Shrewdness, the right contacts,
imagination, yes. At last he put the direct question.

"Did you ever make big money by a stroke of luck, Ikey?"

Brown puffed in silence for a few moments, then removed his cigar and smiled broadly.

"Well, yes, I suppose I did, although I've always told Benjy Cohen, and he tells me, that it was my cleverness. But of course it was luck, really. Does the Six Bars Copper Mine mean anything to you?"

Burnham said that he had heard of it, but in the vaguest way, not even being quite certain where the mine was. He added that he believed it had chiefly stuck in his memory because of its name, which had something improbable about it for a copper mine.

"You F.O. people certainly live sheltered lives," said Ikey. "The Six Bars Copper Mine was, and still is, one of the richest mines going. It's in the Transvaal, but you're right about the name. It was originally the Lagersdorp West. Benjy and I re-christened it after we had bought it. A private joke between him and me."

"I didn't know you City chaps ever joked about sacred things like rich mines," said Burnham. "May I be told the joke?"

"I don't see why not. Sandy McKew's been dead for some years now. But it's a longish story."

"Go ahead."

"It begins a long time ago," Brown said. "You probably remember that I got knocked out in the big German advance in March 1918. Near Bapaume, it was. I was picked up by the Huns and eventually fetched up in a P. of W. lazarett in Eastern Germany. There were about four thousand wounded men there of various nationalities, but only fifteen officers, all British. We had a hut to ourselves, and it might have been worse, I suppose. Half of us were bedridden and pretty bad, at first—the others had broken arms and so on but could walk about. But the only point about the place that concerns my story is the lack of food. For the first four months, until the Red Cross packets from Switzerland and private parcels from our homes began to arrive, we were half-starved. The camp was full of potatoes, growing between the rows of wooden huts, but we never saw a potato on a plate. We had a glass of acorn-coffee for breakfast and a biggish hunk of black bread, very sour and full of grit. This had to last out the day. At noon we had a plate of so-called soup—actually canary-seed soaked in hot water. But the seed remained hard and small, at the bottom of the soup-plate. The water turned pinkish, that's all. Unless we kept back some black bread, we had no supper. I don't know whether you've ever been half-starved? You can't sleep, for one thing. For another, you think and talk endlessly about food. It becomes an obsession.

"At first we used to talk about the first meal we should have when we got home. Most of us chose Simpson's in the Strand—the juiciest roast beef in the world was to be had there. A chef pushed it round the rooms on a trolley, and you chose your slice and he carved it for you. But as time wore on, the craving for sugar, for anything sweet, drove out all other cravings. I've read of the same thing happening to Arctic explorers. I used to dream of a village sweet-shop. But it was the same with us all. To understand my story you must get into your head the extraordinary strength of our longing for sweetstuffs. Otherwise it will sound silly.

"My fellow-prisoners came from a variety of units and backgrounds, and I dare say that at home we should have had very little in common. But living there cheek by jowl, half of us immobile, you can imagine the necessity we were in to get along well together. And we certainly managed to do it. If we sometimes got tired of each other's voices and jokes we didn't show it, and the general good humour, if a bit superficial, was quite genuine. I have forgotten half their names, but I can see each of them as clearly as ever in my mind's eye, and the position of their beds. The only one who comes into this story was a Scotchman called McKew, a perky, red-headed little man from a territorial battalion of the Scottish Rifles. He had a Glasgow brogue and knew everything. A great arguer, but good-natured and not unpopular.

"Now, when food-parcels began to arrive from our homes we

very soon saw that it would never do for each man to consume his own parcel. To those with loving and well-to-do wives they came regularly and were full of delicacies, but to others they came seldom or not at all. So an absolute rule was made and agreed to by all: all edibles were to be pooled and divided equally among us. A grave, capable chap called Munro, who used to stalk about in a London-Scottish kilt, was appointed mess-president, and the drill was for the owner of a parcel to open it himself, abstract the non-edibles, and hand the rest over to Munro. All eyes were upon him as he solemnly made the division on a wooden table that stood in the middle of the hut. Tinned foods, of course, were cooked in bulk, on a rusty iron stove, and scooped out of the pot on to our plates, so many spoonfuls to each man; but sugar, sweets, chocolate and so on had to be counted, or cut on the table, and narrowly we watched him, I can tell you. I remember the first arrival, a packet of granulated brown sugar. There was enough to fill a matchbox for each of us. There were endless discussions as to the best way to deal with a matchbox full of sugar; some put their heads back and poured the lot into their mouths and were done with it. Personally I made mine last out a week—a few grains on the tongue, twice a day.

"As I have said, parcels did not reach us for about four months, and it must have been about midsummer when the thing, to which all this has been leading up to, happened. On a hot afternoon McKew was half-dozing on his bed when Munro, who seldom took a siesta, asked for the loan of a pair of nail-scissors or some small thing which he needed at the moment and knew McKew to possess. McKew, half-asleep, murmured that it was in 'the drawer.' (There was a plain wooden bed-table with a fairly capacious drawer at the side of each bed.) Munro pulled open McKew's drawer, began to hunt for the scissors or whatnot, and saw six bars of chocolate at the back of the drawer. They were those thick, substantial bars that Suchard used to make. McKew had received a parcel from home two days before and had handed over some tins to Stewart, but had said nothing of any chocolate.

"Well, you remember what St Peter thought about Ananias, and how he dealt with him. I believe, at the time, we had much the same thoughts about McKew. Even that irrepressible Scot found nothing to say for himself; he mumbled something about having meant to—having forgotten—but his face was red and he was almost as embarrassed as we were. It's devilish awkward, when you've all been friends together, to discover an Ananias in the next bed but two. The chocolate was duly divided, of course, but there was precious little satisfaction in it. Meanness and deception will take the taste out of anything.

"Well, of course, the thing blew over in time: it had to, in so small and confined a society as ours. About a month before the Armistice we were all 'walking cases' and were dispersed to other camps. By the end of November we were all at home again. About twelve years later my old wounds broke out and I was desperately ill. On recovery I had to go abroad, and altogether I was more than a year away from Cohen, Brown and Company. When I returned to the City, I found Benjy Cohen negotiating for a very big deal indeed. He was proposing to buy, with a view to an eventual public issue, a highly successful Holding Company—the Glasgow Mining and General Trust—which specialised in high-class mining shares. After telling me the whole story he said:

" 'By the way, Sandy McKew, the chairman and controlling shareholder of the concern, tells me he thinks he knows you. Says you were fellow prisoners-of-war in 1918—somewhere in Eastern Germany.'

" 'A little red-headed fellow?'

" 'He's not very tall, and what hair he has is certainly red, but he's hardly little. Fifteen stone, I should guess.'

" 'I remember him,' I said.

" 'A cheerful bird,' said Benjy, 'and seems a nice fellow. Scotch as they make 'em, but straightforward enough.'

"I was on the point of saying 'Ananias,' but I thought better of it. It seemed hardly fair to rake up an ancient story which in any case would sound pretty thin to Benjy. 'Six bars of chocolate in a drawer'—to a man who had never known what hunger was; the tale would have sounded too trivial for words. So I held my tongue.

"Well, in due course I met McKew, and I can't say he showed any signs of remembering the chocolate incident. He was eager to talk about old times and our fellow-prisoners and seemed genuinely pleased to see me again. On the business side, our negotiations went smoothly enough; we found him open and reasonable, and soon had everything tied up. To McKew the deal was an event, because he intended to retire from business on its conclusion. In fact there was to be a celebration dinner somewhere in the West End on the date fixed for completion of the sale.

"A few days before this, McKew, who was always on the move between London and Glasgow, telephoned to me from his Glasgow office to say a small matter had arisen about which he hoped, and was sure, that we could meet him. We were doing a 'package deal' with him—that's to say we were taking over all the securities held by the Glasgow Mining and General Trust, good, bad and indifferent, on a valuation made for both parties by an independent firm of valuers. One of the holdings was of all the shares in a copper mine called the Lagersdorp West, in the Transvaal. Owing to the ore having become exhausted, the mine was about to close down, but there was some cash and good machinery, and we had agreed to pay a smallish sum for these. Now McKew told me, on the telephone, that his people had overlooked the fact that the shares of this company, originally his own, had never been actually transferred to the Trust, and the company being registered in South Africa, it would be a matter of weeks before the transfer could be completed. Rather than delay matters would we agree to leave Lagersdorp West out of the bargain and deduct the agreed price of its shares from the payment due to him on completion? The whole thing was a matter of a few hundred pounds, and I was just about to say 'of course' when something in McKew's voice, heard when he himself was invisible, reminded me of the prison-camp and of 'Ananias.' I felt a sudden reluctance to agree offhand, and I said I would have a word with Cohen about it. McKew sounded faintly put out when he begged me to let him know as soon as possible.

"Cohen, on hearing of McKew's request, said:

" 'Of course. We don't want to hold things up for a small matter like that. I'll ring him up now.'

" 'But,' I said, 'wait, Benjy. There's a thing I never told you, but I think you ought to know it'—and I told him the chocolate story.

"Well, of course, he laughed at me at first. Benjy had never missed a meal in his life, and I had some difficulty in getting him to understand that what Ananias McKew had held back from us had been something of great price—something for which we, and he, had an obsessive craving. He became thoughtful.

" 'It was pretty dirty,' he said. 'But who wants the leavings of a worked-out mine?'

" 'If it really is worked out,' I said.

" 'What do you mean? We saw all the reports, didn't we?'

" 'Only that I have a feeling that once an Ananias always an Ananias. I may be wrong. I hope so. But McKew's excuse for asking the concession is so feeble, if you come to think of it. A delay of a few weeks in transferring a minor asset would be no reason for not completing on the due date. We shall still hold his undertaking to transfer the things as soon as practicable.'

" 'That's true enough,' said Benjy.

" 'Let's just tell him we prefer to leave things alone; that he can transfer the Lagersdorp shares at his convenience,' I said.

" 'I don't quite like refusing him a trifle. Isn't it a bit unfriendly?'

" 'Let's put it to the test, then,' I said. 'Tell him we prefer to leave it as it is. If he accepts that good-humouredly we can write to him later and say that on second thoughts we think his idea a good one. If he makes a great fuss, then there's something behind this and we must insist on the letter of the agreement.'

" 'All right, you suspicious devil,' said Benjy, and called up Glasgow.

"I could only hear my partner's part in the conversation. But it was a long one, and made it quite clear that McKew was fighting for his point as if something really material was at stake. I could see that Benjy was becoming more and more impatient, but he kept his temper, and it was McKew who finally ended the talk by banging down his receiver.

" 'He's not only put out, he's furious,' said Benjy. 'I believe you've got on to something—let's have another look at the Lagersdorp West papers.'

"He rang his bell and asked for the file to be brought. The expert's report on which the Board had decided to close down the mine said, in effect, that as far as present indications went, the workable areas were exhausted and no further deposits had been located.

" 'Hm,' said Benjy, 'I don't think I quite took in those words "as far as present indications go." They may be a mere common form, to safeguard the reporter; but they could mean that the verdict is not to be taken as absolutely final.'

" 'I bet you something's turned up,' I said. 'Ananias has had a cable, you'll see.'

" 'How are we to see if he doesn't show it to us?'

" 'We'll ask him to open the drawer, and promise him that if there's chocolate in it to pay him a fair price. He may want to rob us, but we don't want to rob him.'

" 'He won't have the face, after pretending his suggestion is a mere formality.'

" 'He's had a red face once before,' I said, 'and lived it down. I think I know Sandy McKew. He'd rather have half the chocolate and blush for it than none at all.'

" 'Very well,' said Benjy. 'I'll ask him to run down here and bring all his Lagersdorp papers with him.'

"Benjy got his secretary to telephone the message, and McKew took the night train.

"He turned up at our office the next morning fresh as paint, and in the best of good-humour.

" 'Sorry I was so short with you yesterday, Cohen,' he said. 'I had a lot on my platter at the moment, not to mention a tooth-ache.'

" 'That's quite all right,' said Benjy. 'Now about Lagersdorp. Brown and I have been going through the reports again and we see that the exhaustion of the ore is not quite so certain as we had thought. If there's any prospect of finding more copper after all, we don't want to take advantage of you in any way.'

"I could see a wary look in McKew's eyes.

" 'I don't think that's likely,' he said.

" 'I don't suppose it is,' said Benjy. 'But this report is now four months old. Have you heard anything from the mine since then?'

" 'The usual routine reports,' said McKew.

" 'Nothing about deposits?'

" 'Not to make me change my views,' said McKew.

" 'Then that's that,' said Benjy. 'If there's nothing new, we intend to stick to our arrangement. We'll complete on Tuesday as agreed: you can transfer the Lagersdorp later.'

"I could see the wariness in McKew's eyes turn to anger. But he controlled himself. He even smiled.

" 'It's so untidy,' he said. 'We Scots like to have everything cut and dried. Why not make a friendly gesture, now?'

" 'There's nothing unfriendly in sticking to a bargain, surely,' said Benjy. 'You said yourself the matter was a trifle. Anyhow, we've decided, and that's that.'

"McKew's eyes were no longer angry; they were desperate. I felt convinced that we were about to rob him, which was the last thing we wanted to do. I decided to bluff, for his sake as much as ours.

" 'Why not show us the latest cable from the mine?' I asked him.

"McKew was so taken aback that he blundered.

" 'What do you know about my cables?' he asked.

" 'Nothing that you don't,' I said. 'But it's your last chance.'

"McKew turned scarlet, as once long ago, when Munro took the chocolate from his drawer. But if his pride came before his greed, I suppose a man wouldn't be an Ananias.

" 'I'm in your hands,' he said at last. 'I hope you'll no be too hard on me.'

"Well, as you'll have guessed, the cable was from the mine-manager to say fresh ores had been discovered, as rich if not richer than the former, and apparently in unlimited quantities. Lagersdorp was once again a winner.

"I was about to say, with eyes averted from McKew's, that we should have to come to a fresh arrangement over these shares. But Benjy, who had been studying the cable, spoke first.

" 'This is dated a week ago,' he said.

" 'I forget, exactly,' said McKew.

"The Cohens are nothing if not righteous—descended straight from the Pharisees, I should imagine.

" 'Then you had known for a week what the mine was worth when you proposed that we should let you keep the shares.'

"McKew had nothing to say.

" 'And you pretended that they had no value to speak of?'

"McKew was still silent.

" 'Then good-day, Mr McKew,' said Benjy. 'I think you had better send your Vice-chairman to complete our contract next Tuesday.'

"How McKew got out of the room I don't know. I wasn't looking.

" 'We're making a killing out of him,' I said. 'Is it quite fair?'

" 'St Peter would have *killed* him,' said Benjy. 'The bloody liar. Ikey, you're a genius! You ought to have been a Yid.'

"Of course it was luck, really. But you understand now why we decided to re-christen it the Six Bars Copper Mine."

The Convert

THE little town of Arcaubon, to the cure of whose two thousand souls Father Lascaut had been appointed by the Bishop of Tremblans, lies remote (and unknown, with one exception, to foreign visitors) at the western end of the Maures mountains. Beyond a neat eighteenth-century Town Hall, brown-roofed and green-shuttered, which stands, restful and exact, at the northern end of the Boulevard Foch (formerly the Rue Gambetta) Arcaubon contains little of architectural interest. The Boulevard Foch itself, macadamed throughout its length of two hundred yards, is pretty enough when the double rows of oleanders are in flower, but the huge modern church, domed and misproportioned, which flanks it on the east, is an eyesore to those whose eyes are vulnerable. To the inhabitants, whose eyes are not, it is a source of pride, and the new Curé, who loved nature and humanity, but not art, felt, as its architect intended him to feel, that its bulk alone enhanced the glory of God.

Father Lascaut was an experienced priest and, although not himself a Provençal, after fifteen years in the diocese of Tremblans knew what to expect of his own flock. He expected to find, and found, that the Mayor was a freethinker and the Notary a freemason; that the peasants who flocked into the town on Sundays were more devout than the townspeople, and the women more devout than the men. The one surprise he met with was the exception already referred to: an English resident called Oswold Frogmorton.

Frogmorton, a man in his late thirties, was a member of a respectably ancient Catholic family rooted in Northampton-shire. But unlike his forebears, his grandfather, his father, his uncles, his brothers and his cousins, he found himself, when of age, unable to take any interest whatever in hunting, shooting, fishing, farming, forestry, county affairs or the Bench. Instead the poor fish (as he seemed to his masculine relations) enjoyed nothing so much as sketching, beginning with pale water-colours and ending, when he found these beyond his technical skill, with oils. ("You can't imagine," he said, "the pleasure of discovering that you can paint over your mistakes.") He took lessons from a gifted lady in Northampton who had painted Italy and parts of France from an excitingly bright, not to say gaudy, palette; she fired his ambition, advised "abroad," and arranged for him, on his return, a small one-man show at the Art Circle Rooms in Northampton. His relations and neigh-bours, as easily impressed by a public exhibition as most Philis-tines, and humbly subduing their private tastes under the impact of a laudatory article (by the gifted lady) in the local paper, flocked to the Art Circle Rooms and spent their five, six or even eight guineas on early Frogmortons. Oswold rose in a week from poor fish to talented freak, and felt himself to have a career before him.

But it must be a career in sunshine and under blue skies. The palette he had derived from the gifted lady saw to that. On the other hand his very limited private means forbade much travel or wandering. He remembered Cézanne, went to Aix, found it too expensive and haunted by painters whose skill abashed him explored the countryside on a hired bicycle, and came to rest in the tiny house of a comely widow in the Rue Alphonse Karr in Arcaubon.

He had dwelt there happily enough for something over four years when Father Lascaut took over the parish. The local inhabitants, with whom he rarely spoke, called him *l'Anglais* and forgot him after nine days; he spent his days in painting the hills and olives, those provokingly shimmering trees, restless as the sea, and, after seeing some reproductions of Utrillo, a series of townscapes in the streets of Arcaubon itself. His evenings he spent sipping whisky and water, his one extravagance, preparing canvases for the next day's work, or reading, to improve his French, *Lettres de mon Moulin*. On Saturdays he went to confession and on Sunday mornings to Mass.

Frogmorton, like the rest of his family and most hereditary English Catholics, regarded religion as something you were rather than something you thought about. It was a cause of quiet pride, in so far as it was proof of endurance and fidelity in your ancestors and a touch of well-bred exclusiveness in yourself. Not for the Frogmortons were the polemics and pugnacity on the one hand, the spiritual ardours on the other, of more recent converts. Such parading of the Faith seemed to them unnecessary, even a little vulgar, and had they read, which being squires and sportsmen they had not, the books of those flamboyant banner-bearers, the converted writers, they would have shrunk rather than applauded. On the fifth day and the first Saturday after his arrival, Father Lascaut found himself face to face, in the hideous confessional of the modern Church, with *l'Anglais*, whom he had noticed the day before painting the Town Hall in a style so far removed from that of Utrillo that, had he been able to read the artist's thoughts, he would have been moved to his ever-ready compassion.

Frogmorton, by this time, was fairly fluent in French, although persisting in believing that "*avvy*" represented the sound of the French word "*avez*." His was not an introspective nature and, wholly unsuspecting the multitude of grave sins, mostly of omission, which most of us, however regular our lives, commit, he was accustomed to restrict his confession to a single item : he had slept, during the past week, with his landlady and housekeeper, Madame Lambert.

Father Lascaut was well accustomed to such things.

"For the first time, my son?" he asked.

"Oh no," said his penitent. "For three years now."

"Knowing it to be a grave sin?"

"Of course," said Oswold.

"And you are truly penitent?"

"Naturally," said Oswold.

"Are you going to give it up?"

Oswold was nothing if not candid.

"I'm afraid not, Father."

"Yet you expect me to give you absolution?"

"Father Chaillot always did. I did penance, of course."

"What sort of penance?"

"So many rosaries, so many Ave Marias, so many——"

"But you made no effort to reform?"

"No, Father. You see, we suit each other, and for a man of my age——"

"I quite understand that," said Father Lascaut. "Why don't you marry her?"

There was genuine surprise in Oswold's voice.

"Marry her? It's impossible, Father. We Frogmortons are one of the oldest families in Northamptonshire. We were there in the fourteenth century."

"Madame Lambert had an ancestor alive in the fourteenth century," said Father Lascaut.

It was a new idea to Oswold, and he considered for a moment.

"It's not the same thing," he said. "Or can she prove her pedigree, Father?"

"I doubt it," said the priest.

"Well, there you are!" said Oswold.

"We are all God's children," said Father Lascaut.

"Of course," said Oswold. "But some are gentry, and some are not, and when it comes to marrying——"

"I have had my say. I say no more," said Father Lascaut, who knew the world. "I cannot give you absolution," he added.

"But Father Chaillot——" began Oswold.

"I am not Father Chaillot," said the priest, with a note of severity, "and I cannot give you absolution," he added, "because you have not repented. And the reason you have not repented, is that in your heart you do not believe you have done wrong. Am I right?"

Oswold paused to consider.

"Well, Father, when two people are fond of each other and faithful to each other——"

"You have always been faithful to her?"

Oswold sounded shocked.

"But of course!" he said. "Do you take me for a rip?"

The priest recognised the genuine indignation in his penitent's voice.

"No, my son," he said gently. "You may go in peace."

"But unabsolved, Father? I shan't be able to communicate, or to go to Mass——" He sounded afraid.

"There was nothing to absolve," said Father Lascaut. "Your conscience is clear. I am here to deal with bad consciences, and real sins, not nominal offences. You will find plenty, if you examine yourself. That is enough." His tone was dismissive, and Oswold rose from his knees and left the church with more to think about than had been his lot since he first came to anchor in Arcaubon.

Madame Lambert, who went to confession at a later hour than Oswold, in order to have time to prepare their supper first, also returned full of thoughts. But hers were disturbing ones.

"A funny sort of priest, our new Curé," she said. "Ought we to write to the Bishop, do you think?"

"I liked him," said Oswold. "I've always told you that we were married in the sight of God, and although he did not actually say so, that's what he thinks, I feel sure."

"He did say it to me," said Madame Lambert. "But ought he to have? I shall certainly do Father Chaillot's penances just the same."

"That's your own affair, my dear," said Oswold. Had Madame Lambert written to the Bishop she would have wasted a postage stamp, for he had been well broken-in to Father Lascaut's views about happy, virtuous couples who, for this reason or that, felt unable to go to church before settling down together. The sin, the priest had always argued, was in their coming, deceitfully, to the confessional and there pretending to a wickedness in which their hearts never would believe. And even for that, Father Lascaut used to say, the Church and not themselves was chiefly to blame.

None the less, Father Lascaut had been taken aback by this strange Englishman, a member of his own Faith, who had found no fault in himself beyond that one fictitious sin. He was his parishioner; the little priest was responsible for him, and he resolved to see more of him.

Accordingly when a few days later he again encountered the artist sitting beneath a white umbrella, at his easel, he stopped for a chat, avoided the subject of art, and enquired as to an acceptable day and hour for making a pastoral visit to the Rue Alphonse Karr. There he found Frogmorton sitting, in his best jacket and an unaccustomed necktie, at a small table on which stood a whisky bottle, a syphon, and two tumblers. The Curé sat down and, after the preliminary polite exchanges, was offered a drink. He had never tasted whisky before and welcomed a new experience. His host did not overdo the soda-water, and it was a pretty strong mixture from which the Curé took his first sip. Only his ingrained good manners and presence of mind saved him from making a face. He was a well-read man, and knew that whisky was the beverage which enabled those rugged, dour people the Scots, those wild, dissatisfied Irish, to get the better of the rawness and rigour, or the enervating dampness, of their abominable climates. Having tasted it, he half-admired, half-pitied them.

The object of the Curé's visit was to acquire knowledge of this new sheep of his, and fortunately Frogmorton had poured out for himself a still stiffer peg than that in his guest's glass, with the result that his tongue became loosened, and he began to talk freely about himself. The Curé soon learned, to his surprise, that Frogmorton, after more than four years' residence in Arcaubon, knew next to nothing about the little town or its inhabitants. With the exception of his dear Madame Lambert, he had made no friends and few acquaintances, and those only in the shops where he bought his frugal necessities. It was clear that he lived only for himself, and for his mediocre talent. The Curé listened and sipped, his own spirits sinking *pari passu* with those in his glass, and fell into so deep a meditation as to what to do with this strangely lone sheep as not to notice that his host had quietly replenished, with even less soda-water, the tumbler before him. Not to finish a proffered drink was, in Arcaubon, the worst of bad manners and the Curé, like a good child with his medicine, manfully gulped it down to the last drop.

When he had at length taken his leave, and was walking home, the familiar cobbles seemed queerly distant and his own feet inclined to disobedience. But what disturbed the good man even more was the recollection that when the Englishman had drawn breath, and it had been his own turn to talk, he had embarked, not upon a sympathetic reply to, or commentary upon, his host's remarks, but upon a somewhat unguarded account of himself, past and present. This was so contrary to his pastoral code, and indeed to his whole nature, that he could only impute it to the effect of the whisky.

That evening, after supper, when good food had sobered him and a glass of red wine restored his sympathies, he thought over the whole affair. It was clear to him now that the function of whisky in the unkindly climates of its origin, was to restore to the inhabitants of Scotland and Ireland that good opinion of themselves which their harsh and depressing surroundings were for ever undermining. It was a drink contrived not, like honest wines, to promote conviviality, but to enhance the ego of the drinker. It had been able to compel him, a Christian priest, to talk about himself to a stranger and to come (he blushed deeply at the thought) within measurable distance of a little mild and playful boasting. This train of meditation soon led to more charitable thoughts about the Englishman, whose self-centredness and lack of neighbourliness had so taken him aback. Little as he knew about art, he could not look at the man's canvases without discomfort; the gifted lady's colour-schemes, in the hands of her pupil, positively hurt him. What must the artist himself feel, he thought, about such daubs? No wonder he needed, after each day so lamentably spent, the boost to his ego which whisky could, and did, so effectively give. And how could an ego, after such daily boostings, escape from itself to take an interest in its fellow-egos? Father Lascaut's experience had taught him that the cause of moral shortcomings must be sought, not infrequently, in the body, not the soul. He decided that, while a little gentle prodding in the confessional could do no harm, the key to Frogmorton's sad spiritual condition was to be found in the whisky-bottle.

On the other hand, to deprive his unrepentant penitent of his daily peg, even were he able to do it, which seemed highly unlikely, might well drive the poor man into that state of *accidie* or listless despair, which is so grievous a sin. The remedy lay, he began to see, in another direction. The self-boosting medicine must be gradually exchanged for one that stimulated self-forgetfulness. It would be idle to pretend that the sunshine of Provence, the blue skies, the amethyst hills, the example of the lizards, the aroma of the *maquis,* the cool shadows of archways, of ilex, of umbrella pines, have nothing to do with the pleasant disposition of the people of Arcaubon. "Sunburnt mirth" was not just a poet's fancy. People are merrier in the Midi. But to the unreflecting, which is to say to all but a few of the Arcaubonnais, the influence of all these delights worked far below the surface of their consciousness. The efficient cause of their cheerful and sociable manners was the excellent red wine which they drank at all meals and between them. There is hardly a street in the town without its little estaminet, before which stand plain deal tables and battered wooden chairs with straw-plaited seats. Here sat the inhabitants, morning, noon and night, with a carafe of the good wine between them. To a visitor ignorant of their hours of rising, they might appear to have next to nothing to do. In fact they were laborious enough, but wise enough as well to know that life must be enjoyed as well as endured.

Now good red wine has the opposite effect of whisky, as anyone will know who has tried it. It does not so much exalt as expand the ego, urging it to go out and embrace its fellows. Jesus at Cana knew what he was doing: he was promoting loving-kindness. At every little wooden table in Arcaubon there was laughter, there was sympathy, there were the nods, the expansive gestures, the spread fingers of the extrovert. Even the Curé and the freethinking Mayor could chuckle together over a glass.

So it was to the use of wine that Father Lascaut decided to wean his English parishioner. He began by asking him to call at the presbytery at eleven o'clock in the morning. And there, in the narrow, cool dining-room, where the dark, polished table reflected the squat carafe and the thin-stemmed glasses as in a Dutch still-life, he took the first step in his campaign.

Oswold Frogmorton had grown up terrified of wine. Even when a schoolboy, his father, the Squire, had bidden him sip claret and port with his eyes shut and to say from what Château, from what vintage, the distinguished stuff had come, Oswold never could say. They all tasted alike, and not very pleasantly, to him. His father got cross; he told him that a gentleman must know his wines. Oswold, convinced that never would he know them, trembled for his gentility. It had been the same at the "House" when he went up to Oxford. His fellow-undergraduates knew little or nothing of wines (how could they?) but they looked wise as owls while they sipped them, and made a show of discrimination which again frightened him badly. It ended by his accepting the role of "poor fish", where wines were concerned, as meekly as he later accepted it in the world of hunting and shooting. He decided to have nothing to do with the beastly, complicated, nerve-racking ordeal of wine-drinking. And when he was introduced to whisky, and found that he could readily tell Irish from Scotch, he knew it was the only drink for him.

Father Lascaut, who was observant, noticed that his guest shied a little, putting as it were his ears back, when his glass was filled and fortunately, although never guessing at such a thing as vinophobia, found the exactly right thing to say.

"It's just our simple country wine, without name or year, but I hope you will find it palatable." He had meant it apologetically, thinking that his guest's momentary qualm was that of a man of the world fated with the necessity of condescending. But to Oswold the words "without name or year" had a most soothing and reassuring sound. Here was a glass of wine he could look at unafraid: not only would nobody ask him its name and number; it possessed neither. He felt a novel and enjoyable sense of inner peace as he twined his fingers round the slender stem and lifted the glass to his lips. In his relief he even thought the simple country stuff tasted by no means too bad. His glass was refilled once only, since it was the middle of the morning, but even so Oswold made several remarks about the pleasant situation of the presbytery and even asked his reverend host a few polite questions about himself. It was, from the Curé's point of view, a good beginning.

At next Saturday's confession Oswold, deprived of his stock sin, found himself tongue-tied. For all that he would have been genuinely shocked had he been accused of regarding himself as a man without sin, he was unable, on looking back upon the last week, to remember, in his peaceful life of eating, sleeping and painting, any breach, large or small, of his moral code. The Curé had to prod him.

"Are you sure, my son, that you have committed no sin of omission? How many kindnesses have you done to your neighbours?"

Oswold could think of none, for the simple reason that he had done none. He admitted it.

"Not a single act of kindness? In seven days? In this crowded little town, where many are sick or sorry?"

"No, Father."

"Then, my son, you have sinned gravely. You have broken one of the two great commandments. You must do penance."

"Yes, Father."

Father Lascaut reflected for a few moments.

"Every day in the coming week," he said, "you will treat some fellow-townsman—and I exclude Madame Lambert—to not less than two glasses of red wine, either in private or public. And you will drink two yourself."

"But, Father, I know nobody."

"And whose fault is that?" asked the Curé. "And it isn't even true. You buy your tobacco, you get your hair cut, I have seen you do an errand to the grocer for Madame Lambert."

"Oh, those sort of people?" said Oswold.

"What other sort of people are there in Arcaubon?" said the priest. "There is the Mayor, of course, and the Notary. I will make you a present of both—if you can catch them."

For the first time Oswold, a life-long Catholic, knew the real meaning of penance. His sufferings, until he had broken the ice with the hairdresser, were acute. He had not the nerve to make advances to the Mayor, and he picked upon M. Ragueneau, the coiffeur, because they had already exchanged a few remarks upon the weather during the process of hair-cutting.

Having ruled out the possibility of receiving a tradesman in his own house, Oswold invited the cheerful little man to a neighbouring estaminet. They sat outside, under an awning, in the comparative cool of the evening. The hairdresser was enchanted, and when a Provençal is delighted, he delights. After one glass Oswold lost his self-consciousness. After two he felt at home; after three he let himself go. M. Ragueneau, although no wit, had that admirable substitute, gaiety. Neither talked about themselves, but Oswold learnt an astonishing amount about Arcaubon and its inhabitants. And such of them whose way led them up or down the Rue d'Alsace, where the pair were sitting, soon found a good reason for making a second, and even a third journey down that humble thoroughfare. As the town had been the main topic of their talk, so *l'Anglais*, that evening, was the talk of the town. The number of them who suddenly remembered that they needed a haircut was prodigious, and we may be sure that the coiffeur chattered as he snipped. The Curé, who missed nothing, was much encouraged.

Oswold, on returning home, flown with wine but anything but insolence, had no inclination for whisky that night. He even asked Madame Lambert, to her great satisfaction, to produce a few litres of whatever it was they served at the estaminet in the Rue d'Alsace. Since only one wine was drunk in Arcaubon, she did not have to go so far afield.

On the remaining days of the week Oswold entertained the tobacconist, the grocer, the butcher, the baker, Monsieur Pericaud, the coiffeur's brother-in-law, and Bonifas the postman. On the Saturday the Mayor, whose duty it was to stick a finger in every pie, invited him to lunch to meet the Notary.

At confession that evening Oswold was no longer tongue-tied. He admitted at once that he had hurt many feelings, trodden upon many toes.

"How is that, my son?"

"I forgot to treat Monsieur Bouchetal who sells me turpentine, as well as Monsieur Esquilar at the hardware shop. I'm told that both are deeply hurt. As for little Trottabas, from whom I buy my newspaper, I hear he is heartbroken. He is the only man in Arcaubon, he claims, whom I have visited every day for four years. And it's true. Father; I'm afraid I've been using him as a slot-machine. I'm really ashamed."

"So you ought to be, my son," said the priest. "But you can make restitution. Not less than three glasses for little Trottabas."

"But, Father——"

"Yes, my son?"

"You said I was to do penance. And so it was, until those drinks with the coiffeur. But afterwards it was really quite good fun. You know how it is, after a couple of glasses of this local stuff of yours, one likes everybody and everything. I've really had a most amusing week."

"Loving one's neighbour *is* amusing," said the priest. Oswold was slightly shocked.

"I thought it was religion."

"And why mayn't religion be amusing?" said the Curé. Oswold was still more shocked. As he left the church, he wondered, as Madame Lambert had formerly wondered, whether he ought not to write to the Bishop. But after a glass of wine he decided to do nothing of the sort.

A month or two after that Sunday afternoon when little Trottabas had been lifted to the height of happiness, the Bishop of Tremblans made his visitation to Arcaubon. The Curé's report was much as both had expected. The men reluctant to come to church; the faith of the women and children highly satisfactory; the Mayor a bit of a thorn in the Curé's flesh, and so on and so on.

"All the same, I have made a convert, your Excellency," said Father Lascaut.

"A convert? I congratulate you, my son. What was his former religion?"

"He was a Catholic, your Excellency."

"But how can you make a convert of a Catholic?"

"By converting him to Christianity, your Excellency."

"I don't follow you. Catholics *are* Christians."

"Of course, if you say so, your Excellency," said Father Lascaut, humbly, but looking his Bishop in the face. The Bishop, who knew his man, looked back at him, and detected, in the outer corner of the little priest's right eye, a well-known, a regrettable, an all but imperceptible wink.